Praise for

Chris Lange

Chris Lange knows how to write vampires. She loves them as much as I do because she always wraps me up in her stories from the beginning. Rogan was a dark, sexy, and amazingly gorgeous vampire who was drawn to Liv as much as she was to him. Liv was a woman who discovered the world of vampires quite by accident. Rogan showed her that there was more to her than she ever knew. Enter Raskhan into the story who is King of the Vampires, brother to Rogan, and kidnaps Liv from her world. This begins a tale that is fun to read and is a whirlwind of action, mystery, and incredibly hot and steamy. I didn't want to like Raskhan but I fell in love with him from the beginning. His dominance, teasing, and quick wit won me over. I loved this book...I literally read it in 24 hours. If you love dark, hot, sexy, dominant vampires, I highly recommend this book. *~ Goodreads*

Total-E-Bound Publishing books by Chris Lange:

Gabriel

A TOUCH TOO MUCH

CHRIS LANGE

A Touch Too Much
ISBN # 978-1-78184-588-2
©Copyright Chris Lange 2012
Cover Art by Posh Gosh ©Copyright December 2012
Interior text design by Claire Siemaszkiewicz
Total-E-Bound Publishing

A TOUCH TOO MUCH

Dedication

To my family, for their unconditional love and support.

Chapter One

She never saw him coming.

Liv was opening the trunk of her car when a rough hand grabbed her throat and squeezed. Her heart stuttered wildly, and her lungs cried for air. The hand tightened its grip, just enough to control her, to let her know she couldn't escape. The parking lot looked deserted. At this time of night, even late shoppers had already gone home. There was no one to help her.

She tried to breathe, tried not to panic. Little dots danced before her eyes. A sudden wave of blackness threatened to engulf her. She fought it. But the hand felt strong, very strong. Suddenly weak, unable to think, Liv dropped her bag. It clattered noisily on the concrete, the only sound in the vast silence of the parking lot.

Then...he smelt her. Definitely *smelt* her.

As suddenly as she had been attacked, she was free. She inhaled deeply, sweet air, blissful air invading her empty lungs. She made ragged sounds, her throat burning, her knees so wobbly that she had to lean on the car to ease off the tension. Silly as it sounded, she felt as weak as a freshly-out-of-the-womb kitten. What had just happened? Had he really smelt her?

"Go!"

His voice startled her—only one word, barely whispered, but an order nonetheless. He had assaulted her, out of nowhere. Now he wanted her to leave. The whole scene felt totally surreal.

"Go before he sees you!"

"Who?"

"Some questions are better not answered."

He spoke in a low tone as though he didn't want to be heard. Liv turned around as fast as her still-spinning head would allow her. He stood well away from her, dark, tall, dangerous, his gaze fixed on her. The most attractive man she had ever seen. He had just attempted to strangle her but, looking at him, all she wanted to do was run her fingers through his thick black hair, and touch the hard lines of his face.

Her granddad's favourite curse sprang to mind, as was the case every time she felt troubled or threatened. Holy mackerel, what was wrong with her today? She should already be driving away yet shock seemed to slow her down to the speed of a sleepy hedgehog. Shock or curiosity? Latching onto the mental image of Gramps, she stared at her handsome, disturbing attacker.

"You can't jump on people like that. What do you want?"

She carefully touched her neck, the tender spot right below the chin. Despite her fear and bafflement, Liv couldn't help gaping at him. Who was this man? What did he want to do with her? Rape her? Kill her? If so, he wasn't being very efficient. Why had he changed his mind? Because he had smelt her skin? That made no sense. No sense at all.

"Look, I don't know…"

"Be quiet!"

He had issued an order again, and, in spite of his scary tone, she didn't like it one bit. They faced each other, her still wobbly on her legs, him as hard as iron. She decided not to be impressed by his unnatural gaze and stance, and took a step towards him.

"Stay away from me!" He didn't move a muscle, didn't raise his voice. A gust of wind crossed the parking lot, and his long, black leather coat billowed. A dog's distant howl broke the silence, the sinister sound suggesting loneliness. Liv felt hit by an unexpected lick of desire as she watched the mysterious stranger — a gentle hardening in her stomach, a soft tickle between her thighs.

Although night had settled in, she easily made out his rough features, the strong line of his jaws, the curve of his sensual lips. What could those lips do to her? Slide along her bare skin? Caress her mouth with longing? Kiss the gentle throbbing between her thighs?

Holy mackerel, what was she thinking? She had to quit daydreaming right this instant. For all she knew the man might be the next Jack the Ripper so she'd better stop drooling over him. Yes, good decision.

Maybe she spent too much time in front of the television, but he looked so like a dark knight from past ages, a guardian from a world beyond. Intent on clarifying the situation, Liv took another step.

"I told you to stay away from me!"

There it was again. Did she detect a hint of wariness in his tone this time?

Palms up, she met his gaze. "Why?"

"Because you are the death of me."

Chapter Two

This was getting more and more confusing by the minute. As she opened her mouth to answer him she felt a slight tingle—something akin to gooseflesh, a faint brush of darkness. He must have felt a similar sensation because he finally moved, his eyes scanning their surroundings.

"He's coming. Get in your car."

"Who's coming?"

"Now!"

A deep sense of urgency filled her. Not because he had shouted the last word, but because this peculiar tingle scared her. She quickly picked up the bag at her feet, and went around the car to the driver's door. Fumbling for the lock, fingers shivering, she dropped the keys.

"Go. Now. Go!"

If he was so desperate for her to leave, the best way would be to help her, wouldn't it? Apparently that wasn't on his agenda for he still stood well away from her, studying the shadows.

"Hurry up, he's here."

"Give me a hand then."

The tall, striking stranger faced the main entrance of the parking lot, his whole body as tense as a wire. As he focused on a single point, his jaws tightened, his fists clenched. Half concealed in the near gloom, he looked lupine, a wolf waiting for the fight. While she crouched by the driver's door to retrieve her keys, Liv's uneasiness settled for good.

That was when she saw him.

The other one.

Furtive and silent, he seemed to come from the heart of night. And he looked massive. A huge neck supported an even thicker head, eyes glowering in the dark, distorted mouth showing a long, white row of teeth—a nightmarish vision. Like a monster out of a horror movie. His voice sounded hellish too, loud and gravelly. Like the scrape of a finger on a blackboard.

"What are you doing, Rogan? We've been gone for hours. You should have brought her back."

"Back off, Khord. She's not an A."

The monster called Khord turned towards Liv, to eye her suspiciously. Her nervousness turned into fear under his unwavering scrutiny. If she moved fast, she would have time to start her car, shoot into the night, and forget all about this traumatic encounter. Most of all, forget about a monster who didn't look quite human. Although she guessed he wouldn't simply disappear if she blinked, she seemed to be rooted to the spot.

"Please, go," the gorgeous stranger whispered to her, his gaze never leaving Khord. "You can do it."

He spoke as though he was trying to save her life. Funny twist for someone who had been strangling her five minutes earlier. She knew he was right, though her muscles wouldn't answer her command. The monster approached, moving out of the shadows.

"She looks fresh enough to be an A."

"Stick to your job." Rogan's harsh voice dropped a tone lower. "Let me decide who is viable, and who isn't."

"Yeah, yeah, but what's the harm in having a little sniff? Just a small whiff, hey, what do you say?"

"I say back off!"

The massive man's sudden sneer chilled Liv to the bone. "Don't pretend to be what you're not, Rogan. You know you can't hold your fight!"

"Don't try my patience."

Khord guffawed. He licked his lips like a big cat cornering a mouse. "Come on, you and me—right here!"

The black watch around his wrist beeped. He glanced down and touched it briefly. "Well, seems like it's your lucky day. We have to get back but not before..."

Liv only perceived a blur of movement before the monster grabbed her, squeezing her arm so hard it made her wince. Tears stung her eyes, pain flaring up her shoulder, fear cascading down into her stomach.

Rogan shouted, closing the distance between them. "Enough! I told you she's not an A. Let her go!"

Oblivious to his words, the brute bent his face down to her neck. He smelt her. Sniffed her. Inhaled her. Filled his nose with her scent. And instantly pushed her away with all his might. Liv flew across the parking lot, flew in the dead of night, flew directly towards a wall, and crashed into it.

Except that she didn't crash. Instead she hit Rogan, and fell into his open arms without any sensation of pain. He caught her just before she splattered her brain all over the wall. Then he sat her down on the cold concrete, checking the firmness of her spine. How could he have moved so fast? Impossible, yet she had witnessed it.

Dazed, breathless, Liv lifted her head in time to see Khord staring at her. Wide-eyed, his look of astonishment appeared so intense it was almost laughable. A surprise so unforeseen that she began to wonder what was wrong with her scent. Actually the real issue would be—what did those people *not* want with her?

She didn't have time to ponder the question as the two men rushed at each other.

Such a violent clash—a loud collision reminding Liv of a lightning strike. Khord struck head-on into his opponent, sending him flying away. Instantly on his feet, Rogan ducked to avoid a huge fist, and punched a hard blow in the brute's ribs. He howled, obviously hurt and by now very angry.

A little off balance, he took a step sideways, though not fast enough to dodge Rogan's powerful strikes. Despite his formidable size, Khord went down onto his knees, overthrown by the blows. Rogan kicked him square in the head, only once, and knocked him flat out in a heartbeat. Without a pause, he focused his attention on Liv again.

"You killed him."

Liv thought her own voice sounded odd. Stunned, unable to understand what had just gone on or who these people were, she felt paralysed. Watching Rogan fight struck an unfamiliar fibre in her, and turned him into a dark angel of justice, efficient but ruthless. On a deep level, she also sensed that he had saved her life.

"I wish I had. Yet he's alive, and he won't be out for very long. I'll deal with him later, but you must go."

She stood up then, pushing herself up the wall. Unsteady on her feet, she walked to her car, and opened the door.

"Look, I don't..."

"I know you don't understand. Believe me, it doesn't matter. You weren't supposed to be part of all this anyway."

"I gathered as much, but I'm afraid I need an explanation."

Rogan shook his head and gestured to her. She got in the car, and inserted the key in the ignition. Although way more than intrigued, she knew she needed to get a move on. The weird encounter was over. She should have been relieved, yet she felt reluctant to go. How could she be so terribly attracted to this handsome, menacing stranger?

A long hiss coming from behind them ripped her train of thoughts, a slurping voice following the terrible sound.

"You should never have done that, you traitor!"

Khord seemed to have undergone a drastic change, his jaw hanging at an odd angle, his eyes burning with rage. His features were different too, more sluggish. He snarled, showing the teeth that weren't teeth anymore but vicious canines. As if he had become an animal. As if all trace of humanity had left him. Come to think of it, he looked very much like a vamp... No, that wasn't a real word! In his right hand, Liv glimpsed a kind of gun. Fear spurring her on, she started the engine.

"You can't kill me, Khord. It's against our laws."

Although Rogan sounded sure of his statement, Liv wouldn't have bet on it. Confirming her suspicions, the monster glowered. Wickedness and a deep-rooted hatred vibrated in his voice.

"Yeah, well, I guess the law doesn't apply to traitors like you. You don't know how I've been longing for this very moment, Rogan, when I finally get to blow up that pretty face of yours. What a relief this is going to be. Now say bye-bye, my friend. You die, and I get the girl. But don't worry about her — I'll make sure she ends up where she belongs."

"You'll never get her. I won't allow it."

"Oh, Sir Rogan won't allow it? Who do you think you are? You're nothing but a betrayer!" Khord retrieved a tiny bullet from his pocket. "And this little baby is especially for you — made of silver for your sake."

It all happened in a second. Liv heard the click of a gun, the loud detonation booming around her. She saw Rogan jump in the car next to her, and grunt as he closed the door.

"Go!"

She stamped her foot on the pedal. Tyres screaming, the car rushed out of the parking lot. She swung left past the exit, oblivious of the traffic, determined to reach safety. That was if safety could be found anywhere.

She didn't see any sign of pursuit in the rear-view mirror. Beside her, Rogan seemed in pain, his head lolling with each curve of the road. The bullet had struck his left shoulder. Keeping a firm hand on the wheel, worry causing her to expel rapid breaths, Liv reached out.

"Don't touch me!"

Anger flashed in her mind. After everything he had put her through, he had the nerve to turn her down again. A more sensible woman would have pulled over right there and ditched him, as obviously the man was nothing but big trouble. Why didn't she?

Because, in spite of her reasoning, he fascinated her. Her foot down, she didn't manage to avoid a bump on the road, and Rogan shuddered. Pain probably flaring up his arm, he pressed the wound. Recognising ghastly signs of death on his face, Liv realised it might already be too late for him. Without any way to tell how long he'd last, she asked the question that had been reeling in her mind since he had saved her life.

"You're a vampire, aren't you?"

Chapter Three

Silence. A police siren screeched in the west, a vehicle honked somewhere behind them. As the lights turned green ahead, Liv ignored the freeway. Locked in her car with a wounded, supposedly fictional creature, she wondered if she'd soon wake up from a creepy nightmare. Beside her, Rogan nodded.

"I'm a dying vampire."

"What do you mean? I thought vampires were immortals."

"They aren't. They can be exposed to broad daylight, decapitated, staked in the heart, burnt alive with blessed water, or shot with a silver bullet. Take your pick. Silver is poison to us, and right now it's killing me."

"Sure, but vampires aren't real. I mean I can't believe this crap!"

Although her rational mind still seemed reluctant to acknowledge this distressing possibility, Liv hesitated. Somehow she had known the truth. She just hadn't been able to admit it until Rogan had agreed.

She'd been born into a world where fantasy writers used their imagination to create werewolves, trolls, goblins, shape-shifters, and sometimes hungry-for-flesh aliens from other planets. Those were stories for people craving to live in a fantastic universe. Not real, not real. On the other hand, the dying man beside her seemed real enough.

"Vampires don't exist." She had to state it aloud. Who knew, maybe Rogan would suddenly tell her he had been kidding all along.

"Not in your world, they don't."

"Are you telling me that I'm in some kind of fourth dimension?"

"No." A hint of a smile touched the corners of his mouth, in spite of his pain. "We are in your familiar world, never doubt that, but there are other places, dark places. Trust me, you don't want to go there."

"Places with vampires?"

"I come from another world. No humanity, no sun, no life. Only order, uniformity and extinction."

Caught in the swirl of the conversation, Liv roughly avoided another car coming from the left. Rogan grunted when the sudden jerk threw him against the window. She changed lanes, risking a glance at him.

"How do you survive?"

"What do your legends say?" A weird question, although his interest sounded genuine.

"That vampires feed on blood."

"Then it must be true."

She needed answers, and hoped he wouldn't dodge them. "But if there are no humans in your world, where do you get blood?" As soon as the question came out of her mouth, Liv understood.

"There aren't many vampires left. Ages ago, one of our scientists discovered a Formula called 'The

Solution'. A drop of blood mixed in that Formula and diluted in water feeds everyone for days. All we need is fresh blood from time to time. A single human and our race can survive."

Okay, not a heavy toll to pay. Still, as they needed humans to provide them with food, they had to pick them here.

"How often do you come?"

"About once a month."

One man or woman every month – surely not often enough to alert the authorities and the population about mysterious disappearances. The way Liv saw it, hordes of vampires could go about this business forever without fear of being noticed.

"Why you?"

"Because I'm a hunter."

Taking her eyes off the road for a second, she glanced at the dying creature of the night.

"You hunt people?"

Rogan nodded. "Yes, it's my duty. I didn't choose to be a hunter. I've been gifted with the scent."

"The scent?"

"I can smell the right person just by being close to them. Other vampires, like Khord, don't have that ability. He's a warrior."

Did he mean some people were good to eat and others bad? In his world, did they have five-star restaurants and popular canteens?

"Why do you say the right person? Blood is blood, isn't it?"

"No. For 'The Solution' to be effective it has to be type A blood. All other types are discarded. They aren't poison to us, but they're inefficient, not nourishing. In a funny way, most people don't know how lucky they are. Now, if I'm not mistaken, it's the same for humans. You need to be compatible."

He might have been right, even if the comparison sounded a bit gross. Liv had about a million more questions to ask him. Every fibre of her being shrieked that danger and death sat beside her, yet his story captivated her.

Really? Was she being honest with herself? Was she enchanted by the kind of life he led, or by the way he looked and moved? Or by the powerful sensation she had experienced when he had caught her in his arms?

"Where are you taking me?" Rogan asked, his hand pressed on his shoulder wound, his features distorted with pain.

Although unsafe for her, Liv had an idea. Still she had a mile to make up her mind, so she decided to dodge the question for a while.

"I admit I don't know my blood type, but you told your friend I wasn't an A. So, why did you attack me?"

"Khord isn't my friend." Rogan's growl sent a shiver down her spine. "Don't ever make that assumption again."

She kept silent, waiting for the answer.

"I was misled. I was hiding in the shadows when you got to your car, watching you, taking in your scent. At first it seemed you smelt like an A, but not quite, so I decided to clear the matter up. I never imagined you could be pure blood. I realised my mistake too late. Only when I touched your neck and started, well, you know…"

"Killing me?"

"I never intended to kill you." Rogan's deep sigh might have been a groan of pain, yet he carried on.

"It's just that unconscious bodies are more convenient to transport."

This time, Liv didn't want any more gross details. Maybe later, she'd ask him where he transported bodies.

"Do you often make that kind of mistake?"

"Never. Not once. But how could I have guessed you were the...?" His voice trailed off.

"The what?"

From his tone, she sensed that a vital piece of information was coming her way, like an impending doom. Edgy, hands gripping the steering wheel, she waited until out of the corner of her eye, she saw him subsiding against the window. Rogan had passed out.

When they reached their destination, Liv shook him out of his slumber. Although kind of groggy, he let her help him up the steps before she closed the front door behind them. Once in the foyer, he watched his surroundings, his gaze guarded and wary.

"Where are we?"

"Home."

As soon as she spoke the words, she felt his body harden against her, and his arm stiffen around her shoulder.

"It's too risky."

"Why? Is he coming after me? How is he going to find me anyway? He isn't psychic, is he?"

"No, but he'll get help and I won't last very long. I can feel my strength waning. What will you do with my body?"

He spoke in such a low voice her stomach tightened. Liv had known him less than an hour, and to say the least his intentions remained unclear, yet she didn't want him to die. Then again, what could she do about it? All she had going for her was positive thinking. Not much in the face of death.

"You won't die. You just need to rest for a while."

Rogan grabbed her arm. He might be in agony, but his grip on her still felt strong.

"Don't kid yourself, there's no time for that. I'll be dead in a few minutes."

As if his words weren't dreadful enough, he squeezed her arm to hammer his meaning home.

"Ouch! You're hurting me."

"Sorry."

He let go of her arm before taking off his long coat to get a close look at his injury. The bullet had deeply pierced his shoulder, tearing flesh, and the exit wound felt cold to the touch when Liv brushed shaky fingers on it.

When he had crossed the foyer into the living room, Rogan lay down on the couch, his strained expression signifying the end had come for him. White as a ghost, gaze feverish from poison, face contorted with pain, he closed his eyes like a man who had given up.

Obviously, the silver had quickly invaded his body, slaying one of the not-so-immortals in its wake. When Liv approached him, he opened his eyes to take hold of her hand. Back in the parking lot he had been so adamant that she should not touch him, the natural gesture surprised her.

"How come you're not afraid of touching me anymore?"

"Doesn't really matter now, does it?"

He flinched with pain, his body weakening from the deadly poison. His speech quick and ragged, he then revealed his suspicions, all the while holding her hand.

By now, Khord should have guessed who Liv really was, along with the threat she represented to their race. Although he had been defeated for a while, he wouldn't let it go. He'd come after her because that was his duty as well as his nature. Not only would the thick-headed brute be back to finish the job, but he might also bring back-up.

In spite of his degrading condition, Rogan seemed reluctant to tell her the truth. Considering that she couldn't figure out what he was talking about, she wondered why. Yet he obviously felt her life had been endangered, and he made a final attempt at warning her.

"Listen to me."

Subjected to his solemn stare, Liv knelt on the floor right by his side. Their hands joined.

"There is an ancient legend among my race. It says that on the dawn of Doom's Day, vampires will rule the world. All the worlds. But a great enemy will stand in their path. He is One and Only. He is named the Bringer of Death. He is pure, invisible, and his touch is lethal."

Rogan paused. Inhaling with difficulty, he seemed to be summoning his last strength to end the story.

"I've never believed in that legend until today."

Their eyes met, truly connecting for the first time. Shuddering with a sudden feeling of dread, Liv swallowed to ease the tension in her throat. Yet when she heard his statement, the itchy lump sank all the way down to her stomach.

"You are the Bringer of Death."

Chapter Four

"What are you talking about?" Despite Liv's usual cool composure, the words dropped out of her mouth like pellets of lead.

"You are the enemy of my race. The One and Only who has the power to wipe us all out."

Somewhere during the ride back home, the man must have lost his mind. Either that or the silver had had more effect than just killing him.

"You're mad! How can you say such things? I don't have any power, I'm just a woman. And guess what..." she added as the thought crossed her mind. "I see my face in the mirror every day, and I'm not invisible."

Rogan had either fallen deaf or pretended not to hear her protests because he kept going, his intakes of breath coming less and less frequently.

"You're invisible to vampires. It means your blood has no category, no scent. Of course they can see you, but they are unable to smell you. If you were standing in front of an army of vampires, they wouldn't take a second glance at you. Only the best hunters could apprehend your true nature."

As he talked, he stroked her hand with his fingers. She reckoned that he was trying to soothe her, or help her the only way he could.

"That's why I stayed away from you in the parking lot. I couldn't recognise your smell. It confused me at first because each human has a blood type and a scent. You didn't seem to. It was all totally unexpected and intriguing. I had to think fast. I don't know why this old legend popped into my mind, but it did, and I realised I had touched the Bringer of Death. Beyond a doubt, I was going to die on the spot."

"Stop calling me that!"

He had gone mad. The poisonous silver must have insinuated into some hidden corners of his brain, rendering him delirious. Whatever he believed in, he had no right to dump his problem on her, and she couldn't listen to any more of those lies. She might be gullible at times, but not enough to embrace the dying vampire's delusions.

"That's enough! I don't want to hear —"

She didn't finish her sentence, for Rogan had passed out again. Unmoving as a stone, face ashen, his body lay rigid.

Holy mackerel, he was dead. No, no, he couldn't be dead, not him. He was too strong, too good-looking to die. That wasn't meant to be. It could not be. And somehow the fault was hers. Dear Lord, it was all her fault.

Tears brimming in her eyes, Liv gently brushed his hair, her fingers tracing the bridge of his nose, the line of his mouth. Like a priestess from dark ages, she prayed.

Come back, please come back to me.

From the core of her being, something shifted — a colossal force of nature seeking freedom, desperate to be let out. Liv stayed still. She listened to the deep, regular beat of her heart, the slow pulse of her blood, the long whisper flowing in her veins. She kept quiet and expectant while a sudden rush lashed out its power. Then pure instinct took over.

She applied her hand to Rogan's wound. Eyes shut, focused on a rising, unknown sensation, she felt the force bolting into his body, a tremendous energy penetrating his every fibre. Time stopped. Dizziness loomed over her. Tiredness opened its jaws.

All at once, the force retreated. Worn out and quivering, Liv unstuck her hand. Rogan's wound had disappeared. She saw skin, intact and healthy, through the bullet hole in his clothing.

She had just healed a vampire.

* * * *

The healing had taken a toll on her. She remembered dragging herself to the armchair, and she must have fallen asleep at some point because she opened her eyes at the sound of his voice.

"You're so beautiful. What's your name?"

"Liv."

Fully awake, the vampire stared at her. She straightened up, glad that she had only lit a small lamp on the table.

"How do you feel?"

"I feel fine."

Of course he did. After the 'what in the hell is happening?' treatment she had given him, death had nothing to do with him any longer.

"Maybe you should rest a little."

"I don't need to rest. What I need..." In mid-sentence, he stood up with graceful ease to bring Liv to her feet. "What I need is this!"

As he took her face in his hands, a fiery tremor of desire went through her. She held her breath, waiting for the first intimate touch, the first caress of passion. But he made no move.

He just held her, his dark golden-freckled eyes drilling into hers. Under that unperturbed stare, her heart missed a beat, her insides froze. So close to his masculinity, she felt herself craving for his touch, for the raw feel of him. Still he made no move.

Eyes locked, infused by a hungering thirst, she suddenly relinquished every scrap of rationality she had ever possessed. Human and vampire joining as one? Well, so be it! Ever so slowly, he drew nearer, a fraction of a move—a tantalising instant born from mutual lust.

His lips touched hers, gentle as the soft brush of a bird's wing. When he pulled back, the longing for him twisted her guts. Frustrated, imprisoned in his embrace, she wished for more, so much more.

His sensual gaze fixed on her. He put his mouth over hers again. She wanted this second to last forever, wanted to melt against his unyielding body. But he started kissing her, his lips awaiting hers, as if in search of her taste. So strong, alien, and unexpected, the sensation took her by surprise, causing her to sway on her feet.

Then she felt his tongue parting her lips, entering, penetrating her mouth. His deep caress shook her whole world. Seemingly impervious to her intense emotion, he reached inside her, opening her up, as if he had all the time in the universe. As if nothing else existed, he kissed her, bringing her towards an abyss of unknown territories.

He dug his hands into her hair, immobilising her head. Heat swelled up in her. Long, hot shivers of excitement blazing hard, her wanton mouth making love with his, their tongues entangled, ensnared. They licked and sucked until she couldn't stand it any longer. Until she thought she would surely faint from hunger. Passion was becoming their master. Passion was enslaving them, and there was no turning back from it.

He drew away from her.

"Liv!"

Her name on his lips brought her back to reality, and it felt like dropping from heaven. Although he stood inches apart from her, she felt empty, alone in a life without his touch.

"No, don't stop."

"Liv, I must!"

She lifted her arms behind his neck to press her body against him. A dark ripple crossed his eyes, a pitch-black shadow from another realm. In spite of his denial, Rogan clutched her with vigorous arms, halting her breath. Whispering through clenched teeth, he looked torn. "You have no idea what you're asking. You don't know what I could do to you."

And he kissed her, the rough kiss of a man swept by desire. He probed her mouth with his tongue, creating vivid, electrifying vibes she couldn't have thought possible. He was hard against her, captured in the intensity of the moment, his arms feeling like steel around her. Yet she sighed when his hands found the soft curves of her body under her clothing.

He grunted as if her moan unlatched something wild in him. Without a word, he got rid of their sweaters. Muscles tensed, he looked about to go in search of the sensation of bare skin, the feel of her fullness against his chest. But he didn't take her in his arms, and she felt naked, utterly exposed to him.

Seemingly drowning himself in her eyes, he traced the round contours of her shoulders with deft fingers, slipping down her sides, reaching the firmness of her stomach, smoothly rising up to her breasts. She breathed heavily, a scant flush of modesty warming her cheeks.

Standing in the centre of the living-room, only shadowed by the pale glow of the lamp, the vampire caressed her. He appeared riveted to her body, and deaf to anything that wasn't her.

She moaned when he touched her nipples with tender, slow motions. Pressing, rolling, releasing. Twisting, wrapping, releasing. It was bliss and torment. She had no grip on herself, no handrail to hold onto.

A voracious fever gripped her, carrying her into the furthest recesses of her womanhood. Under his lascivious, slow fingers, her heart leapt, her blood ran, her intimacy pulsed. Right up to the point where she thought she would dissolve, possibly turn to melted cream.

Driven by instinct, she flattened against him, brushing her breasts against his bare chest. Her mouth found his, kissing him with flaming eagerness. He enfolded her tightly in his arms, their lips attuned, their tongues entwined. It seemed the kiss would never cease, never come to an end.

But Rogan recoiled. As abruptly as he had embraced her and pressed her hard against his body, he let her go. Although his eyes were cloudy, he spoke in an unwavering voice.

"We can't do it!"

"Why? What's wrong?"

"We can't. That's all you need to know."

His implacable tone didn't leave any room for hesitation. Baffled and speechless, Liv stared at his icy, perfect face, realising his decision had been made. She had never felt so cold.

Chapter Five

Getting dressed had been quick, laced with a good dose of embarrassment on Liv's part. Standing half-naked before the man who'd almost stolen her thoughts, then pushed her away didn't call for self-confidence. But what on earth had made him change his mind? Something wrong with her? How could he kiss her so profoundly, then turn away in the middle of it? Could he not see the woman in her instead of the Bringer of Death?

Sure, that had to be the reason. Rogan had lost himself in her for a brief moment, but awareness of their dangerous situation had dawned on him. Even if she had healed him, he still thought of her as some kind of enemy. For him. For his race. But what could she do about that? As much as she desired it, there might not be a way out.

Liv switched the lights on in the kitchen, feelings of anger and frustration washing over her. In some way, he had let her down, and she needed compensation. Maybe a sweet, hot coffee would ease her bruised emotions. Opening the nearest cupboard, she got her favourite mug out. Intending to heat it up in her new microwave oven, she was pouring cold coffee into the mug when she heard a light shuffle behind her.

"Liv."

His low voice didn't hold any trace of embarrassment. When she turned round, he leaned against the kitchen door, looking at her, at the way she moved.

"I have to leave."

"Sure, go." The need to brag pulled stronger than reason. Deep down, though, she already missed his presence, already knew she wouldn't be able to forget him — nor his hands on her body.

"I know you're angry."

"Angry? Is that what you think? Well, let me tell you something. You're nothing but a selfish, arrogant brute, and I regret the minute I laid eyes on you. Hang on! Actually, I didn't. I was too busy fighting for my life, wasn't I? So, Mister Vampire, do you still think I'm angry?"

She hadn't meant to lash out at him, but too late the words blurted out of her mouth, unleashed by her fury. "Then you come in here, in my home, waiting for what? For me to save your life? And guess what? I do!"

"Thank you for that."

Ashamed of having desired him way more than he had desired her, furious with his cool composure, she didn't even hear him. "What else did you expect? A woman in your arms to complete a good day's work? Well, I almost did that too, didn't I?"

"Shush, you aren't —"

"Don't you shush me," Liv shouted, pointing her finger straight at him. "Don't you dare shush me. I'm so exasperated with you right now I could easily become that Bringer of Death of yours. Come to think of it, I'm positive I'd enjoy that. Please, don't tempt me!"

"Liv, calm down."

She ignored his attempt at peacemaking, as well as the palms of his hands raised towards her. She'd been bragging again, yet her vivid feeling of betrayal rapidly turned into fury. She had no intention of stopping there. He might be a deadly vampire, and he might be able to kill her in a wink—however, she couldn't care less. She needed to vent.

"If I decided to destroy you, there's nothing you could do about it. Because I am your greatest enemy, and you're afraid of me."

Hearing her words somehow conferred on them a significance. The brief spark in his eyes also told her she had hit dead centre. Without pause, she sneered at him. "You, Rogan, the best hunter of your race, are afraid of me!"

In two strides he stood in front of her, gripping her hair with one of his hands. A finger under her chin, he lifted her face to his, and kissed her so completely that her anger vanished.

All she could feel were his lips raking hers, his tongue invading her mouth, his fervour so agonisingly delicious she felt on the verge of fainting. He wasn't afraid of her in the least, never had been. He was a fighter, he was a survivor. Dominating her, violating her tender mouth, he led her to an awareness of her true desires, a carnal place she now longed to uncover.

Too soon, Rogan released her. Out of breath, limbs trembling, Liv put a hand on the kitchen table to catch her balance. For now she could only look at his dark, menacing eyes.

"Be careful, Liv. Don't go too far with me!"

His hungry tone sounded almost like the snarl of a wolf. He had said something similar to Khord just before cruelly smashing his face to the ground. Yet seeing him moving like an animal, lithe and untamed, Liv couldn't help feeling aroused, even more so as he uttered a simple statement.

"You saved my life. I am grateful for that, but I'm warning you. I will not take another scolding."

"Don't you like me a little bit?" she murmured like a child, big tears brimming in her eyes.

All thoughts of rebellion left her. She couldn't fathom his character or his motives, and she was tired of being left in the dark. Up to now, she had always taken pride in being a strong, determined woman. Now her world had gone down the drain, and she was left with a vague sense of fragility. Wiping a tear under her eye, probably seeing her vulnerability, Rogan smiled for the first time. And the glory of that smile touched her heart.

"So that's really why you're angry with me? Because you thought I didn't like you."

Piqued, she tried to show off, knowing he'd never fall for it. "I'm not angry anymore."

He sighed. As if he couldn't decide on the best way to convey his thoughts, he banged his fist on the table. The sharp noise resounded in the kitchen, and showed his opinion better than any words could have done.

"If I could make love to you right here on this table, I would. But I can't, and you have to take my word for it."

"No, I don't. I'm sorry, but that's not good enough. Don't get me wrong, I want to believe you. It's a little too confusing, though."

Liv figured her comment would gall Rogan, but his expression softened. No anger there, no irritation, just patience.

"It isn't an issue I'm allowed to answer."

"Allowed? By whom?"

"That's not important."

Dismissing the subject with a wave of his hand, he lightly stroked her hair.

"I have to go. I need to locate Khord, and stop him before a bad idea gets into his thick skull."

The way he said it didn't bode well. Enjoying the touch of his fingers on her hand, Liv nonetheless couldn't help feeling apprehensive. Anxiety making her voice quiver, she stared at the dark vampire.

"Do you mean he might be looking for me? Can he find me?"

"He saw your face in the parking lot, so I guess he could identify you if you crossed paths. However, he doesn't know anything about you. He's got no name, no address, nothing. That should give me ample time to change his perspective."

Liv had to suppress a shiver when a cunning light glowed in Rogan's eyes. Knowing that Khord might already be coming after her wasn't her idea of a wonderful time. Hearing that Rogan would leave her alone didn't exactly agree with her either. Yet, as much as she'd have begged him to stay, her pride stopped her. She had always dealt with life so far — she'd carry on. Her worries lay elsewhere. She had witnessed Khord's amazing strength and fury, and, in a way, she felt more anxious for Rogan.

"Be careful, will you?"

"Don't worry about me. I can take care of myself."

Tall and handsome, he stood before her. Although letting him go distressed her, thinking she might never see him again, never touch him again was almost too much too bear. On top of her powerful attraction, the intimate moment they had shared made it all the more difficult.

"Maybe I can drive you somewhere."

Indeed, a feeble excuse to stay around him a while longer. But pressed by time, she couldn't think of anything better.

"It's all right. I'm fast."

"But you're hardly recovered from your wound. Besides, my car is fast, too, and it's no bother."

She left the kitchen before he could reply, and came back with her handbag. Rummaging inside for her car keys, she only took a few seconds to proudly dangle them in front of his eyes.

"See, no bother at all. We can go any time you want."

Instinct taking over, Liv paused. Something felt wrong. Brow furrowed, she looked inside her bag, riffling through the most familiar object she owned.

Rogan touched her arm. "What's wrong?"

"I'm not sure. Hold on, let me—" She swiftly emptied the contents on the kitchen counter to go through them. Without any care, she discarded a crossword book, lipsticks, pens, tissues and purse with jerky movements until the main part of the bag contained nothing but dust.

"Oh, my God!"

"What is it?"

"My wallet's missing!"

Rogan's body hardened, but he didn't say a word. He didn't have to. Somehow, Liv could figure out his thoughts. Trying not to babble, she recalled the fateful moment.

"In the parking lot, I dropped my bag. I was scared, I picked it up. I knew something bad was coming. I didn't check. I should have, but I didn't. Then that monster turned up. I was so scared. Oh God, oh God, he's got my wallet, my name, my address!"

Torn between fear and self-resentment, she began shaking when Rogan took her hands in his. Although he whispered, she knew his touch was meant to soothe her as much as to drive his words home.

"It's okay. Don't be afraid, I won't let anything happen to you. Listen to me. We're going back there now. Maybe he didn't see your wallet, but we have to make sure of that. All right?"

Sensing hope, her anxiety abated. He appeared so strong and self-possessed that she felt comforted, protected, safe. With him by her side, the world's harshness and unforeseen pitfalls seemed to fade to a distant dream. The impression of bravery she had felt filled with caused her to nod.

"If I'm unlucky and he knows where I live, we can't stay here anyway. Oh my God, what did I do?"

She had spoken in a soft voice, yet she hated the notion of her home being endangered. The living room she had furnished. The bedroom she had decorated. The kitchen she had spent happy times in. In spite of reason, she had the haunting feeling she would not see this place again. Rogan's hand held hers. Liv let out a long sigh.

"I'm ready. Let's go!"

The front door banged open.

Chapter Six

In the blink of a vampire's eye, Rogan disappeared into the living room. Following suit at her own human pace, Liv went to the kitchen door. With great care, she attempted to hide behind it and to see what was happening in the other room at the same time.

"Tss, tss!" Khord hissed, holding her wallet, waving it to and fro. He had his vampire face on. He looked repulsive. "Seems like someone left this behind. Thank the lady for me, Rogan, will you? She made my life so much easier. A bit daft, isn't she?"

"Why are you here, Khord?"

Rogan must have been biding his time, in the hope of finding out about the brute's intentions. At least that would've been a sensible approach. Liv listened behind the kitchen door.

"What do you think? Spend a few hours sunbathing by a pool." He laughed at his own stupid joke.

"Considering you look fresh and that it took you long enough to get your ass here, I'm guessing you went home. Of course you did!" Rogan slapped his forehead as if just remembering something obvious. "Some of us need to be refreshed, don't we?"

"Shut your big mouth!" Khord spat the insult, not looking in the least amused now. "I'll get you for that!"

Liv couldn't fathom the exchange between the two vampires. Which home were they talking about? The place where they dwelt with other vampires? And why in the world would they need to 'refresh'?

Intrigued by the mysterious conversation, she peered through the small gap between the frame and the door. Intent on not missing a single word, she almost lost her balance when Rogan continued.

"I bet you didn't tell the council you shot me. The penalty for murdering one of our race is death. So what did you tell them when you went back without me? That I got lost in a parking lot?"

"I had nothing to say until I was sure you were dead, but they're wondering where you are. They might send a search party."

From the little Liv had learned she reckoned Khord hadn't worked out who she was. He had merely been wary of her because he hadn't been able to catch and identify her scent. Rogan had been right, Khord didn't seem gifted—only a stoic, experienced fighter without brains.

As safe as her guess might be, it also meant the council Rogan had just mentioned were still unaware of her existence. Was she supposed to feel relieved? Come to think of it, probably not, given that a search party was on its way. How long before they realised they should find her and Rogan? Just as the idea started whirling in her mind, Khord tilted his head, his demonic features making Liv want to cringe.

"Tell me, how come you ain't dead? My bullet was a killer."

"I'm a lucky guy."

Contorting his horrid face, body tensed and ready to fight, Khord threw the wallet at his opponent. Rogan ducked, avoiding the flying object with ease. It banged against the kitchen door, and fell at Liv's feet. Going down as quietly as she could, she grabbed it, aware of Rogan's sarcastic tone.

"Oh, you missed."

"I'm gonna kill you. For good this time."

"Come on, my pet." By all means, Rogan seemed to enjoy the dreadful encounter immensely, his voice and choice of words beguiling Khord. "Show me what you've got!"

The monster rushed at him.

Liv observed the whole scene from her hiding place, open-mouthed. Sometimes she was able to perceive one of them striking at the other, sometimes all she could see was a blur. Like an imprint of a thunderbolt on a retina. She heard the grunting, the clash of blows, the cries of pain, the insults from Khord's foul mouth.

Chairs crashed on the combatants, paintings dropped heavily from the walls, the table seemed to lift itself, then went down with a loud thump. As it was still night-time, Liv didn't want to think about the neighbours. With any luck, they were into deep sleep, not phone in hand and ready to call nine-one-one.

Instead, her reaction to the vampire feud amazed her. Without a doubt, her heart beat for Rogan.

Standstill.

Challenging each other from across the room, the vampires had stopped fighting. Poised and sombre, Rogan had his hand pressed against his side. Khord held his left arm, out of its socket. His right leg featured an odd angle too, his toes facing his body. His nose looked broken, flat on his face. He seemed in a very bad shape, much worse than Rogan, and Liv could have swelled with pride.

"Why are you protecting her?" Khord gurgled between clenched canines, face distorted with rage. "What is she to you?"

The monster's watch beeped. Unfazed, Rogan glanced at it before adopting a jeering tone.

"Go home, Khord, it's time. And get a mirror on your way, you're a real knockout!"

Fury bloating his voice, the repulsive hulk spat blood. "You'll pay for that. You heed my words, Rogan, you'll pay for that!"

Grabbing his right leg, he twisted it roughly. Without even wincing he applied the same treatment to his arm and nose. The ensuing snapping noises were sickening, raising bile in Liv's mouth. When Khord had finished reconnecting his joints, Liv thought he could have passed for human once more, provided that he wore a balaclava on his head. As he trudged back towards the front door, he pointed a crooked finger at Liv.

"I'll tell about her. You'll see. They'll come for her."

Then he was gone.

"We have to move!"

No hesitation in Rogan's voice. She gathered he knew what was coming, and wanted them both out of the way. Liv feigned not to notice the wreckage when she stepped into the living room.

"Are you hurt? What's going on?"

"That swine isn't lying. He will inform the council about you. They're going to send a tracker."

A wave of uneasiness rose up her arms. Liv rubbed her sleeves. "A tracker? Is it different from a hunter?"

"Yes and no. A tracker is a highly trained agent, picked from the best hunters' teams. He's first initiated, then immersed in the ancient art of tracking. Practicing can get tough but when the training is over he's capable of finding anyone, anywhere. Once he smells a scent, he can track it down anyplace. All he needs is an item the person has touched, usually fabric. No matter the distance, no matter the time. Sooner or later, he always gets his prey."

"Is he coming for me?"

She must've looked scared because Rogan rushed to take her in his strong arms. She leaned on him, shielding herself from a fateful future. As if aware of her inner turmoil, he held her until the fear quieted, giving her the reassurance and the strength she needed. He traced her lips with one finger.

"Nothing will happen to you. I'll keep you safe."

"Why would you do that?"

It seemed a reasonable question to ask. At first he had regarded her as smelly food, now he was appointing himself her guardian. Unsure as to his change of heart, she looked at him expectantly.

"Never mind that! Let's get out of here, I don't have much time." He pointed at the window. "Sunrise is in less than an hour."

He let go of her so she could retrieve her wallet and handbag. Outside, she locked the front door, gave the car keys to Rogan, and eased herself down on the passenger seat.

"Drive. I know where we can hole up till sunset."

They raced with the approaching dawn, traffic still being light. Less than an hour later, they parked in front of a worn-out motel. Coloured a deep, dark blue, the sky awaited imminent golden rays of sun. Getting out of the car, Liv cocked her head towards the square building.

"The motel belongs to my best friend. I guess it's not much to look at but it's private."

Sandra was doing some paperwork while listening to the radio full blast. As Rogan announced he felt exhausted and needed the room right away, she handed him a key. He took off in a hurry, leaving the girls to chat. Only when he was gone did Sandra turn the radio down.

"Sorry about the racket, I love this Christian Kane. He's got such a sexy voice, I wouldn't say no to him."

In spite of the dire circumstances, Liv had to grin. "You'll always be my favourite 'I behave like a teenager' friend. In a way, you haven't changed a bit since high school."

"Yet you love me just the way I am." Sandra's smile beat hers by a good margin. "Now enough of me, how have you been since Christmas? More importantly, what are you doing here so early? Have you been thrown out of your flat? And sweet Jesus, who's this hunk of a guy?"

"A friend in trouble. He needs a hand."

Peals of laughter escaped Sandra's lips, and creased her forehead. "I'm sure he does." As if a funny idea had crossed her mind, she added with a hint of glee, "Is his wife jealous? Is she going to storm in here?"

"Look, Sandra, it's not what you think. I can't explain now, but I promise I'll tell you everything later."

"Are you going into his room?"

"Well, yes, but—"

Mirth barely controlled, Sandra held up her hands. "Okay, okay, it's not what I think it is. Listen, I'm off at three today. Tom's doing the afternoon shift. Come round if you want a little chat."

Although Sandra seemed to be having great fun, Liv felt sure she could count on her. After almost ten years of close friendship, neither of them had ever let the other one down.

"Thanks for everything, Sandy, you're a good friend. I may drop by later, but we don't want to be disturbed this morning. It's been a long, tiring night. I'm beat, and rest is in order."

Eyebrows raised, Sandra displayed another grin of complete understanding. "Sure, darling, enjoy your nap!"

Only in front of the motel bedroom did Liv realise the innuendo in Sandra's words. Shaking her head, she let herself in.

Rogan had already drawn the heavy drapes shut, cutting himself off from the bright, glorious rays spreading from the east. The room was cloaked in darkness but not so much that Liv couldn't well discern his silhouette stretched out on the big double bed — one bed only.

Did he usually sleep during the day? For that matter, did he sleep at all? His golden eyes following her every move as she dropped her bag on the nearest chair. Liv succumbed to the relentless question circling her mind. *What are we going to do now?*

Chapter Seven

Rogan's intense gaze never left her. Liv felt nervous, also weary and unclean. As he didn't say a word, she went to the bathroom, in need of a long shower. The hot water soothed her tension, and helped clear her mind. She wanted to ask Rogan so many questions she didn't know where to start, the main one being what was going to happen.

Drying off, she felt much better although still tired. Small wonder her face looked pale when she glanced in the mirror. *Too bad!* She stepped into the bedroom, intending to have a small rest. The thought of dressing in her rumpled clothes didn't appeal to her in the least. But when Rogan saw her come out of the bathroom with only the towel coiled around her, he sat up straight, features strained.

"What do you think you're doing?"

"Getting ready for bed. Come on, scoot over. Make room for me!"

Was it her mischievous tone or her attitude that left him speechless? Whatever the case, he just watched her closing the distance. Only when she had almost reached the bed did he react.

"Don't!"

"What's wrong?" Liv spoke as if walking around wrapped in a bath towel was the most natural thing in the world. "Oh, you mean, my new outfit! You don't mind, do you?"

Frustration and anger fought for dominion on his harsh features. He pointed to the bathroom door. "Go get changed!"

Dear God, how she enjoyed watching his distressed face. Shaking her head, she took another step towards the bed. "What's the matter, Rogan? You aren't attracted to me anyway."

Although she didn't see him move, he was suddenly standing next to her. Taking her arm, he carried her along to the bathroom. "Damn it, woman, I'll teach you manners!"

Swept along, Liv had no choice but to loosen her grip on the towel. As it fell soundlessly on the floor, the vampire halted. He let go of her arm, his dark eyes devouring her nakedness. Breath caught in her throat, heart racing, she felt split between fear of his sudden stillness and excitement at being contemplated in such a spellbinding way.

"Hell...no!" he heaved.

She was crushed against his body. His kiss urgent and demanding, he consumed her with his mouth while he ran his hands over her back, over the roundness of her buttocks. Holding her waist, Rogan bent down to trace searing stripes with his tongue, from her neck down to her breasts. He slowly licked her nipples, compelling them to rise, compelling them to stiffen under his erotic touch. He sucked, fondled, and tasted her skin, using both lips and hands to arouse her erect buds.

Sucked in a whirlpool of drifting and staggering sensations, Liv had never felt so intensely desired. His caresses driving her wild, she hung on to him, to this powerful man who carried her towards her most savage fantasies. In a flash, he laid her down on the bed.

Rogan sat beside her. He trailed his hands all over her body, his eyes riveted to her nudity. He caressed her as if she was a long-awaited treasure, a beautiful pearl to be cherished.

"Rogan, I want to see you."

Their eyes met. Liv could see a barrier in his, a careful protection from a concealed menace. She didn't move, simply held his gaze. A man and a woman bound by the most natural law of the universe.

Then he seemed to make up his mind. He stood up and undressed to reveal his muscular body, to display his beautiful, arrogant craving for her.

Keeping her voice soft, eyes riveted on his hard-on, she raised her hand. "I want to touch you."

His body covered hers. Hungry, they united their mouths in a long, sensual kiss. Liv stroked his back, feeling rock-like muscles under her fingers. She lazily explored his skin, the luscious sensation of his manhood pressing on her belly. When her nails bit into the firmness of his buttocks, a quiver coursed through him.

He groaned. A true male, he shifted his body, wanting domination. She was ready for him, feeling his hardness brush against her thighs, moving to her humid opening, fondling the delicate flesh with agonising slowness, holding back to the point where her need became an obsession, where she moaned to be roughly possessed.

Overwhelming hunger gnawing at her raw senses, Liv coiled her legs around him. Following her instinctive move, he braced himself and pushed his head in her neck.

"Please, Rogan. Oh, please!"

At the sound of his whispered name, his whole body tensed. Abruptly, he rolled away from her to bury his face in the pillow. Although muffled, his words rang clear.

"I'm sorry, I can't. I thought I could, but I can't. Not with you."

Numbness overcame her, like a defensive shroud safeguarding her mind from intense frustration, intense rejection, intense emptiness. Yet, above all this, she felt extremely hurt. Too hurt for blame. Much too hurt for anger.

After a silent minute, he got up and put his pants on. No words would come out of her mouth when he turned round and watched the tears flowing down her cheeks. She must've been the very image of pain because the sight of her torment seemed too much for him to bear. On impulse, he knelt by her side, taking her hand in his. He looked distressed by an inner affliction he was dying to soothe.

"We can't do this."

Liv pushed his hand away. His mere touch inflaming the hurtful dismissal that couldn't be quite shaken off, she covered herself up with the sheet, and closed her eyes to blot him out. The tears wouldn't stop. But she had to observe him through her eyelashes.

He clenched his fists, stood up and started pacing the room. The way he moved gave her the impression he felt completely at a loss.

Sighing, Liv opened her eyes. "Tell me."

He didn't have to ask what she wanted to know, did he? No, he had gone too far this time. Yet he looked reluctant to speak the truth. Why? For fear of devastating her? For fear of losing her? That didn't make sense.

"Tell me now."

"The last thing I want to do is hurt you. Making love to you would achieve exactly that."

"Why? I'm not made of glass."

"Because..." Rogan faltered. Pausing by the edge of the bed, he looked at her in a funny way. Like he feared she was about to flee? Sure, she couldn't figure out his odd attitude, but she wouldn't allow him to avoid a straight answer. She wouldn't falter.

"Have you ever been with a human before?"

He nodded.

"Did you hurt her?"

"No."

He resumed pacing the room, his trouble obvious. His dread for what could happen to Liv hardly disguised.

"So why would you hurt me?"

"Those women were different from you. They were just women I had sex with, and I never felt compelled to be with them. Well, not like with you. If I did, I'd have sent them away. I always assumed women to be the same, but I was wrong. You're special. You are the Bringer of Death."

"Do you think I could kill you?"

Palms up, Rogan shrugged. "If our ancient legend is to be believed, your touch is lethal. I guess you could."

There they were again, back to his obsession with a ridiculous Bringer of Death. So far and in spite of their touching each other, Liv hadn't killed him. As a matter of fact, she had saved him.

"How come I healed you then?"

"I'm not sure but I believe it's because your blood is pure. You're one of a kind."

Eyebrows raised, curiosity piqued, Liv sat up, sheet tightly tucked under her armpits.

"For real?"

"Never mind that." He dismissed her question with a quick wave. "Your touch isn't what I'm wary of."

Liv tensed. Watching his dark brows and stiff body, she had the sudden, uncanny feeling that what was coming would shatter her dreams, her illusions, possibly her life.

"I'm listening."

"Are you sure you really want to know?"

"I'm listening," she insisted. If she had told him she was an alien god masquerading as a woman, he wouldn't have looked more disheartened.

He complied. "Suit yourself." Rogan sat on the edge of the bed. His eyes were mesmerising, golden freckles shining in black liquid.

"It's powerful, it's compelling, and it's irresistible. It's a violent impulse we cannot fight. Twice with you I've tried to restrain it, but it's much stronger than I am. Twice I have failed."

He extended a finger to her face, the simple gesture bringing into play the sleek muscles of his shoulders and arms. "You are so beautiful, so adorable. I know full well you're my doom, and I don't care."

His thumb touched her lower lip, his eyes fixed on her. As if he couldn't be stopped, the words flowed out of his mouth. "I want to take you in my arms, to kiss you long and hard, to touch you like you've never been touched, to give you the pleasure I feel running in your veins. If only I could do all those things, I don't give a damn what befalls me. But I swear I will never harm you."

Listening to the rise of his tone, Liv sensed the time for revelation had caught up with her. Although caution should have been foremost in her mind, she was hooked on his every word.

"In the heat of passion, vampires bite each other."

It came back to Liv in a rush. When she had whispered his name, when she had almost asked him to take her, he had sunk his head against her neck. And she had felt two pin-pricks on her skin.

Those had been his fangs.

Chapter Eight

Liv slept for the better part of the afternoon. Stunned by Rogan's revelation, she had needed time to absorb it. She had dressed and gone out for a bit of fresh air before coming back to nibble at some sandwiches and snacks from the vending machine. Afterwards in the stuffy, dark, tightly sealed motel room, they had both fallen asleep.

When she woke up, the day had to be kissed goodbye. Rogan sat in the single armchair, watching her, awake, alert, and handsome beyond belief. Liv straightened up and placed a pillow behind her head. Despite everything that had gone on, sleep had rested her mind and body.

"What time is it?"

"There's still an hour till sunset."

Good. A full hour should be sufficient to hear the rest of the story. Rogan hadn't yet told the whole tale, but would the end upset her as much as the beginning? Time to listen and see.

"Tell me about your race."

"Vampires used to be humans. It is said in our ancient prophecies that God turned a man into the first vampire to punish humanity for its sins. As a result he was condemned to feed on his own former kind for eternity. Never to see the sun again. He roamed the Earth for a long time, alone, drinking from his prey to survive, and killing them. One night, he got careless. He fed on a human, and left her for dead. Unfortunately, she wasn't quite dead. The next day, she had become a vampire."

"That's impossible. I'm not an expert, but it's common knowledge humans don't turn into vampires unless they also drink their blood. Well, that's what I've always heard anyway."

Rogan smiled dismally. The muscles of his arms tensed as he leant forward to shake his head. "Believe me they do."

"How?"

"A toxic fluid in our fangs. When we bite, it seeps into the blood. If we don't kill the prey, the deed is done."

Gross, so gross. A little disgusted, Liv didn't need a movie screen to picture the pain and terror some humans had had to endure in the past. Yet, if creating vampires proved that easy, there should have been millions or billions of them around. All things considered, humanity should already have been eradicated. So, what had gone wrong?

"Does it mean a new race was begotten?"

"When the number of vampires increased, humans became conscious of their existence, and of the subsequent danger to them. Various inaccurate accounts were told, later written, evolving into myths with the passing of time. You know, myths are usually true but rarely right."

"What happened then?"

"The vampiric population grew and grew to the point where war was unavoidable. We may have great speed and strength, but humans possess something very special indeed – stubbornness. They quickly understood we were immortal, but not invincible. By sheer force of arms and will, they drove the vampires out of this world. No prisoners. They slew many, and banished the rest into a place we call the Overworld."

That must've been where Rogan had come from, the other universe he had mentioned once. Although Liv would have loved hearing all about this mysterious Overworld, she knew they may not have time.

"I'm guessing no humans escorted vampires over there, so how did they feed?"

"First, councils were constituted. As the Dividing War had taken a heavy toll on both sides, humans and vampires made a truce. Besides, the Formula had just been invented, so they agreed that a portal between our two worlds was to be left open to ensure the survival of my race."

"A portal? Who created it, and how?"

"I'm afraid this knowledge has been lost with time, at least on your side. Although we need to keep it open, strict rules were dictated. Only hunters and warriors were allowed through the portal once a month by way of a transportation device."

Raising his arm, Rogan showed her the watch on his wrist. Liv recognised the peculiar object at first glance.

"Khord has the same watch. I heard it in the parking lot, and also at home. Why did it beep?"

"Because I'd spent him. He was drained. The laws of nature are somewhat different in the Overworld. We are bound to these rules, just like you're tied to your laws. Here we're less efficient, and prone to weakness.

The watch is also an alarm to tell us when it's time to be refreshed."

"What's that?"

"An immersion in a tank of Formula. Even diluted, human blood is still a source of great strength for us. Actually it works like a battery, and a few hours in the tank are usually sufficient."

Okay. If Liv had her facts right, vampires fed on a drop of blood every now and then, mostly stayed in their Overworld dens, and needed to rush home for a check-up and a long soak when their watches rang. Interesting! Yet the handsome vampire by her side didn't appear to abide by the same rules. What was different about him?

"Rogan, you've been in my world for almost twenty-four hours. You don't seem to need refreshing."

"I never do. I don't know why—it could be a flaw of nature or a very rare disease in the vampire ranks. Our scientists have been researching my case, and they haven't found out the cause either."

Like she was supposed to be different, could Rogan be special in his own way? After all, her touch should have killed him, not saved his life. As much as the idea needed some pondering, Liv wanted to know more about the brute who had trashed her apartment.

"Khord came after me. Do you mean he's a hunter?"

"No, he's a warrior assigned to protect his partner if need be. Warriors and hunters always pair off when it's time to cross over and find nourishment. I got Khord yesterday, not my lucky day!"

His face remained impassive as he stated the obvious. Without pause he went back to the subject at hand.

"After the truce, we needed some kind of order so the council established a system resulting in three divisions—the civilians, the warriors, and the hunters who can specialise in tracking."

"I'm amazed. I had never heard about all that. I find your story very hard to believe, even if the war occurred a long time ago."

"The knowledge has been either lost or forgotten because the human mind doesn't like, let's say, complications. It's much easier and more convenient to keep believing vampires are nothing but fictional characters."

He might've been right. Another universe filled with blood-suckers purchasing walking food did seem frightening. Wouldn't it be so much better to deny it, and to forget about it after a while? Probably, but the forgetting didn't solve in the least her immediate problem.

Every time he moved, Rogan reminded her of a solitary hunter, a dark animal ready to pounce on prey. His very animality aroused her way more than any man ever had, and keeping his sex out of her mind was getting more difficult with each passing hour. At the cost of startling him, she had to make him understand she didn't fear him.

"You won't bite me."

Although Liv had spoken in a hushed tone, Rogan looked taken aback for a second. Only for a second, then he was standing right beside her before she had a chance to see him move from the armchair.

"I will. With you, the impulse is overwhelming, impossible to contain. I tried, but to no avail."

"If you did bite me, what would happen?"

The words had barely left her mouth when Rogan's lean features froze, and his unwavering cold look scared her for the first time.

"I would have to kill you, or you'd turn into a vampire."

Chapter Nine

Sunset.

As soon as Rogan was able to step outside, they avoided the reception hall and headed straight for Liv's car. Moving away from her familiar places appeared to be the safest course of action for the time being.

A few vehicles were parked in front of the motel, but nobody seemed to be hanging about. Very conscious of Rogan's hand wrapped around her forearm, Liv walked with him to her car. As she opened the door and dropped her bag on the seat, a rough tone raised goose bumps on her arms.

"I'll be damned if it isn't lover boy and his new girlfriend!" Khord guffawed, his voice coming from the shadows.

Liv felt Rogan's arms around her, then a sickening whoosh. Next thing she knew, she found herself in an empty warehouse at the back of the motel, concealed behind a stack of cardboard boxes.

"Stay here!"

With that, he was gone.

She stayed put for a few seconds, a little queasy from the super-speed trip, heart beating too fast. Yet she was no man, and curiosity soon won over. Keeping a low profile, she edged quietly towards the entrance.

Both warehouse and motel were surrounded by fields on all sides, so she had an open view, lit by the rising moon. The dark border of a forest loomed in the west. Khord and Rogan stood facing each other, two bloodthirsty predators expecting the call of battle.

"How did you find us?"

"The council sent a tracker to her place this morning shortly after you left. He picked up your scent, and traced you here. By then it was almost dawn so he had to get back, but I knew where to find you two."

"Looks like you used your brains for once!"

Eyebrows tight together, Khord raised a huge fist.

"Shut the fuck up! You're nothing but an outlaw now. The tracker reported to the council. He told them he was unable to pick up the woman's scent so they want her for analysing."

"I think you're lying. You know as well as I do that no human is allowed in the Overworld."

"They'll make an exception for her. From what I've heard, Zontag wants her real bad. Who's gonna know anyway?"

Khord might well be close to the truth on this one. Liv's disappearance would be noticed, of course, but not for a while. Plenty of time to get probed, analysed and eaten by vampires. Unless Rogan protected her. Concealed behind boxes, Liv watched his fighting stance.

"She isn't going anywhere."

"You don't have a say in the matter. I'm taking her back."

"Sure, it's not like I've already beaten the crap out of you. Twice, if memory serves."

As Khord sneered instead of blowing a gasket, Liv reckoned he hadn't laid down all his cards. Holding her breath, she shuddered when she heard his triumphant tone.

"Who said I came alone?"

Liv suddenly spotted the second warrior coming out from the shadows of the motel. Although she didn't think he had seen her, she kept completely still, her heart pounding hard.

They might not kill Rogan on the spot, but they would take him back to their world. Chances were they'd hand him over to the council, question him, lock him up, maybe torture him or sentence him to death. She'd never see him again, and she didn't want that. God, no, she didn't want that.

But who was she kidding? Yes, she feared what might happen to her, yet that wasn't the main reason, was it? Too late to deny the truth, now she had to open her eyes. She had feelings for him, feelings for a vampire. And the icing on the cake came down to a simple fact—they couldn't even make love. No way would they ever be man and woman. Wasn't that ironic? Wasn't that every woman's dream?

Realistic and hurtful as the thought was, she didn't have the leisure to dwell on it. She and Rogan were in a deadlock all right, but she had always relied on her instincts. She'd find a way to right their situation.

Khord and the warrior encircled Rogan. A blur of movement, a shift of dark colours the eye couldn't quite catch. Sighing, Liv wished they wouldn't do that, wouldn't use their terrifying speed to confuse her. To prevent her from ensuring Rogan was still unhurt.

She heard the mighty blows, but not being able to see was terribly frustrating—until the sounds ceased and the image stabilised.

Although on his legs, Khord appeared to be totally disjointed but already focused on the task of snapping his bones into place. In the process of getting up his partner didn't look in better shape, yet seemed still determined to get his quarry. Rogan lay flat on the ground.

"No!"

Liv's shout tore through the stillness of the night. Rogan was dead. He had to be or he'd get up and start fighting again. Fight for both their lives. Disturbed by her cry, a cloud of bats flew away. Swinging his head round at the sound of her voice, Khord yelled to the other warrior.

"Get the girl! She's in the warehouse."

"What about him?"

"He's out. I'll deal with him. You get the girl, and take her home. The council is waiting for her."

"Okay."

With a last, loud crack, the warrior locked a bone back in his shoulder. Without hurry, he started walking to the disused building, obviously confident no speed was necessary. His prey was only human, and a woman at that. Meanwhile, Khord grinned at Rogan's motionless form lying at his feet.

"Well, lover boy! Not so boisterous now, are we? Where's your sense of humour? Passed out? Gone down the drain? Doesn't matter 'cause this time you're coming home with me."

Guffawing, he bent over to get Rogan.

Chapter Ten

Liv didn't even contemplate outrunning the warrior dispatched to get hold of her. Hidden behind the boxes, she figured her best bet remained to stay put. She could see Rogan through a small gap between boxes. That was all she cared about, much more than the anguished voice in her head telling her the gorgeous vampire had been killed.

Heart filled with lead, she observed the nameless warrior as he walked into the warehouse. Since the building had been shut down, the place had become a real jumble of garbage, cardboard, containers, and out-of-order equipment lying around. Of course he wouldn't be very long locating her. All she could achieve now was to buy some time.

Khord grabbed Rogan's wrist, without doubt in an attempt to activate his watch. When their limbs met, the disgusting hulk was lifted off his feet, and thrown away at full force. The landing sounded brutal. The impact must have jarred his freshly mended bones, and sent waves of pain through his body, because he uttered a sharp cry while drawing his fangs out.

Relief made Liv quiver when she saw Rogan propelling Khord, and bending forward to pick something off the ground. For the first time, she laid eyes on his vampire face. Unlike Khord, he hadn't turned into a monster. Fangs out, taut skin shining golden in the moonlight, powerful jaws set to rip and kill, Rogan was the most handsome and virile creature ever.

When Khord looked up, Rogan was on his feet, battered but frighteningly in command. Liv perceived that something about him rattled Khord. His stubborn, aggressive stance? His unwavering gaze? Or the determination on his face? Whatever it was, an untold dread seemed to be creeping into Khord's mind, blunting his courage.

"Get up! Let's get this over with."

Rogan didn't look like a fighter anymore, but more like a hunter on the brink of slaying his prey. He had grabbed a chunk of wood from a pile of old debris, no doubt intending to stake his enemy.

Although in bad shape, Khord couldn't resist flouting.

"Ain't you gonna save the pretty bird? Guess not, it's too late for her."

Though he scoffed, he was only to be crushed down again. Razor-sharp fangs glittering in the bright moonlight, Rogan jumped on Khord. Pinned to the ground by Rogan's weight, the brute watched the lethal vampire lift his arm, stake pointed at his enemy's heart.

Khord's words acutely ringing in her mind, Liv forgot all about her pursuer, and shouted.

"Rogan, don't! If you kill him, they'll sentence you to death!"

She was brutally flung sideways, and she crashed into boxes. Half full of junk, they nevertheless cushioned her fall. Using her hands as brakes, Liv slid on her back towards the entrance of the warehouse. Before she could take another breath, the warrior was already holding her down. Immobilised, dazed, she felt his hand seize her wrist to fasten a watch around it. The device to send her into the Overworld. The vampires' world.

Holy mackerel! Panic flooding her veins, legs kicking nothing but air, arms trying to escape the iron grip, Liv cried out. She knew her shout wouldn't help, knew her flailing would only delay her assailant for a few seconds, but she couldn't just lie there and let him take her away to unknown whereabouts. No, she didn't want to go to the Overworld.

She glanced outside. Looking like he hated this strange universe made for a weak race, Khord seemed to be mustering his strength. Whatever he planned, Rogan out-thought him with an unexpected move. He dropped the stake, and pressed a button on the brute's watch. Khord vanished.

Too far away, and unable to see her as the warehouse lay in shadows, Rogan wouldn't be able to rescue her now. She had only herself to rely on, yet herself wasn't going to be enough. As he squeezed her wrists so hard that tears sprang to her eyes, Liv finally realised the end had come for her. Closing her eyes, she addressed a silent prayer to the vampire who had made her heart beat with lust and love.

And it came. An instinctive power infused her body, causing her to open her eyes in a rush. Like a destructive force demanding to be let out, the unrelenting sensation gave her an order. Overwhelmed yet trusting her instincts, Liv obeyed.

She wrenched one of her hands free and put it on the warrior's chest.

Facing outdoors, she saw Rogan on his knees looking towards her. She heard him calling her name, heard him yelling at her to stop. Impossible. Too late. Although vibrating from the violence of the energy raging inside her, Liv still knew she didn't want to stop. And why would she? While she kept on staring at Rogan, the corners of her lips stretched up.

"Bite me!"

She pushed. The invisible force reached its peak, and rushed out. Impacted. Penetrated into the vampire's body. Soundlessly. Without stirring a breath of air. But nothing changed. Incredulous, Liv cast a glance at the warrior. Apart from the fact that he had stopped trying to put the watch on her, he hadn't moved. As far as she could tell he simply seemed a bit at a loss, the watch now sliding from his fingers to fall on the concrete floor.

Without even a whoosh, Rogan stood by her side. As he shoved the other vampire aside, the weight on Liv's stomach disappeared instantly. Helping her to stand up, his threatening vampire features stirring a wanton need in her guts, he commanded the warrior.

"Go home if you don't want to die!"

The soldier nodded while striving to find the right spot on the watch he was wearing. He disappeared. As soon as the warrior was gone, Rogan's face shifted. Fangs retracted, his golden eyes glowing in the darkness, he looked like the Rogan she had stumbled upon in the parking lot, sombre and handsome. Drawing Liv to him, he carefully took her in his arms to brush a lock of hair from her forehead.

"Are you all right?"

"My back hurts a little, but I'm fine."

"What just happened?"

The feel of his hand on her hair soothed her, and turned her on at the same time. Would she always react this way to him?

"I'm not sure, Rogan. I felt something in me, like an incredible force running in my blood. I don't know how to put it except that it wanted out. It begged to be let out. At first I thought it did, but something went wrong I guess. Anyway, nothing happened."

"I know, Liv, I saw it in your eyes. I had the impression something had taken you over. You looked…"

He didn't finish his sentence, seemingly getting a grip on himself, or putting a troubling image out of his mind. So close to him, she couldn't dismiss his odd look as a trick of the moon's silver light.

"How did I look?"

He let go of her and bent down to retrieve the watch the nameless warrior had struggled to fasten around her wrist.

"Forget I said that."

"No, I won't. What were you going to say?"

"We can't stay here. As soon as Khord has reported, the council will send others. Come on, let's get the hell out of here."

"Rogan!"

Frustrated with his obvious refusal to answer her, she almost shouted his name. He must have sensed she really meant to get it because he fiddled with the watch, and let out a long sigh.

"You looked like a goddess of justice, utterly gorgeous and impregnable. An iron maiden feared by men and vampires alike. Watching you, I felt…"

"How did you feel?"

"Excited. Compelled. And, oh hell, so aroused. You dig up my worst feelings, Liv, and you don't even know it!"

That was when she noticed his body still tense and hot from battle, his feverish eyes alight with inner lust. As he talked, his face seemed to revel in the moonlight, his teeth slowly drawing out. Face to face with the vampire of her dreams, Liv understood there was no going back this time. Her voice as soft as a silken thread, she reached out to touch his fangs.

"I know you'll never hurt me."

He swept her into his arms.

Chapter Eleven

Rogan had stretched out his long coat on the grass. Liv smelt the rich damp soil, the thick fresh odour of growing plants. Over their heads a canopy of trees curtained them, but she could see a myriad of stars shining bright in the sky. One for each beat of her heart.

Entwined, their naked bodies glistened in the moonlight. Rogan had buried his strong hands in her hair and was now kissing her breasts adoringly. She relished the weight of his body, the heavy pressure increasing her desire. When he licked her nipples — his provocative tongue flickering on the pink skin — she raved from pleasure.

As he nibbled her, she felt him stiff between her thighs. So stiff she couldn't think of anything else. Nothing existed but this willing hardness, solely intent on getting inside and ravishing her with delight. That wasn't fantasy. That was rock-solid proof of his need of her. He ran his tongue over her breasts before whispering her name.

The throbbing between her legs wouldn't abate. Calling. Demanding. Frantic for the man's skin grazing her opening. Abruptly, Rogan let go of her hair. Leaning on his forearms, he raised his head to look into her eyes. When he spoke, his strangled voice sent shivers down her belly.

"Liv, the impulse... It's coming!"

"Let it come. You won't hurt me."

She gasped when his hard sex touched her for the first time. Really touched her. He pushed himself in, just a little, and stopped. Skins blended. Fluids mixed. Legs splayed, heart pumping blood and desire, Liv panted under this agonising sensation.

"God, Rogan!"

He gave another push, penetrating her moistness. She thought her whole body was liquefying, dissolving into the purest emotion she had ever known. She quivered, tremors of irresistible pleasure running their powerful course. Breathing hard, eyes closed, she let her senses take control.

"Look at me!"

She obeyed his harsh command to discover anew his beloved face marked with passion. As their inflamed gazes met, he slid all the way in. She moaned, her chest quickly rising up and down, her attention fixed on his sensual mouth. Then he whispered for her.

"Look at me! I want to see the joy in your eyes."

He slightly withdrew, only to drive himself hard into her. Submitted to this excruciating motion, she dug her nails into his shoulders. Wild tears gushed out, wetting her cheeks, sliding down to her lips. Never had she felt so much pleasure, so much desire for another man. Except that the term 'man' couldn't be applied in his case. He was a creature of the night.

He rammed her even harder. She shuddered under his total domination while his grunts brought a pleasure she hadn't anticipated. From head to toe, she needed to be mastered, to be the servant of his steamy cravings. She hadn't been prepared for anything remotely like this enslaving sensation. She wasn't sure her heart could take it, yet she begged for it.

"Love me, Rogan."

He murmured her name, suddenly tightening his grasp on her. In a single swift thrust, he impaled her. She cried out. Huge and rigid, he filled her completely, giving her what no other man could give her.

He drank her cry with a passionate kiss, all the time gliding in and out of her, again and again. Legs widely spread to fit his every strike, powerful waves of delight already drowning and engulfing her, she got goose bumps when he moaned in her ear. Moaned from the relentless pleasure they were sharing.

Then he straightened up, his broad chest pale in the moonlight. He placed his hands on her hips to pull her forward and backward, all the while staring at the rapture he must be seeing on her features, on the curve of her mouth, in her eyes widening with his every thrust. From her ecstatic look, he must've known she wanted it.

Attuned to his intensifying rhythm, she arched her body, her round breasts rising, demanding he went deeper into her. He responded immediately, his hands sliding on her buttocks to bring her to him in hard motions. She watched his fangs come out, she heard him groan.

"Liv, it's so strong!"

He looked like a golden god—a god of war, of wild passion, of eternal love. Sensing he couldn't restrain his instinctive impulse any longer, she pushed her hair back to offer him her bare neck.

"Do it. Do it now!"

He lifted his face to the sky, and let out a feral cry. He then leant down to her in a wolf-like manner, mouth wide open. When she felt his fangs on her neck, she arched her back even more, in unison with his movements, coupling her body with his vigorous thrusts.

He might turn her into a vampire. He might have to kill her. At that precise second she didn't give a damn one way or the other. Because what she felt for him was now too complicated for words, so much more powerful than lust. She craved the feel of him inside her, the feel of his piercing fangs against her throat. Acting on her raw emotions, she brutally clamped her inner muscles around his stiff rod. He grunted. He shivered from head to toe.

And it happened. The pain when he bit into her flesh. The wetness of her blood. The power of release jolted their whole bodies, shocked their beings, staggered their minds. A sensation so extreme, she felt it submerged them and united their souls in ecstatic agony. They climaxed together, their screams ripping the cloaked silence of the woods.

Chapter Twelve

They walked out of the forest without a word, for no words were needed. He had licked the blood on her neck, the deep punctures stinging hard. With a single bite he had marked her forever, and she rejoiced in it.

Just by looking at him, she knew he feared for her. For tomorrow's dawn. For his race chasing her. For each night apart. For each day he wouldn't be able to protect her. Now she had to leave behind the places she enjoyed, the people she loved. Without looking back. Now she was on the run for her life.

Holding hands, Rogan and Liv walked to her car. Although night still ruled their side of the universe, time was running out. As she opened the driver's door Rogan pushed a lock of her hair back, and stroked her cheek. Then his features stiffened.

"I can't come with you."

Her throat tightening, Liv grabbed the hand lingering on her cheek. She squeezed the strong fingers before looking at her new lover, at the vampire who had blown her peaceful world to pieces.

"Why not? You said I had no scent. If it's true, how will they be able to track me?"

"They won't, but trackers will smell me."

He made sense. As much as she would have liked him to be wrong, he had thought this through. If they stuck together, his race would find her soon because of his own scent.

Yet as logical as it sounded she buckled at the idea of being left alone, of moving about in dangerous territories on her own. Without him to protect her, she'd be unable to rely on his presence, strength and courage. Although she believed herself to be rather strong and resilient, she really didn't want to face a horde of vicious vampires alone. Rogan felt confident they wouldn't go after her. She didn't.

"Shit, Rogan, I don't want to be alone. Please, don't do that to me. What will I do? I can't even go back home. Where will I go? Does it mean I'll never see you again?"

He placed a finger on her lips. Aware she was fighting off a rush of fear, he cupped her face, his gaze getting hold of hers with no option to slip away. She stood perfectly still, mesmerised by the brightness in his eyes. When he spoke, a chill ran down her arms.

"I'll find you anywhere."

The certainty of his words and the confidence oozing from his voice caused her to shiver.

"How?"

"Because I bit you and tasted your blood. Because you're the Bringer of Death, yet you healed me. Or because…I love you." Rogan pressed her hand against the hard muscles of his stomach. "I'm not sure why, but now I can feel you inside. Wherever you are, I'll always know."

Lapping up everything he said, Liv inhaled loudly. Way too frightened of his imminent departure to perceive whatever he was feeling inside, she licked her bottom lip. But when her fingers bore down on what felt like a marble slab, she gazed at his sensual mouth and knew she wasn't mistaking lust for love. Not anymore.

Their lovemaking had changed everything. His biting her under the protective canopy of trees had called forth deeper feelings. His licking her blood and tasting her essence had bound them to one another. But holy shit, she loved a vampire!

Seeming to experience the same emotion, he brought his lips down on hers, taking the breath out of her. As they joined, she moved both hands around his back while he embraced her, their bodies finding each other again, hungry with desire.

Had she ever been kissed so intensely? Could it be called passion? Sure, she had read about this wild sensation in romance novels and she had watched lovers exchanging perfect kisses in movies, but that was make-believe. Not real. As for her ex-boyfriends, compared to this overwhelming feeling, they had merely been pissing into the wind.

He crushed her against him until she believed her bones might snap, and made love to her with his tongue. Her instincts responded to his hard-on. Desire pushing her to moan, she clutched him even harder as if their bodies could penetrate each other.

Liv almost toppled over when Rogan finally let her go. Eyes slightly elongated and burning bright, skin taut over his cheekbones, he looked halfway through transformation.

"Hell, Liv, I can't control myself around you!"

As he cursed, his face shifted back to its human form. Soon only a fierce glow in his eyes still testified to his craving for her. A shiver went through him as he straightened up and took her hand.

"The next couple of days will be harsh, and I wish I could be there for you. But I know you're strong enough to make it."

"What do you mean?"

"You're a vampire now. By tomorrow evening you'll feel thirsty, your body yearning for blood. Try to hold it off as long as possible. I promise you I'll do everything I can to be back before you have to…"

His voice trailed off, his gaze leaving hers to stare into the night. For a second he seemed to have gone to a faraway place where darkness ruled. Watching his serious air, Liv realised his sinking his fangs into her flesh would have unavoidable consequences — already had.

Holy mackerel, she had become a vampire! Fighting off a wave of nausea, she took a deep breath to clear her mind. If Rogan couldn't speak the dreadful words, she'd say them for him.

"Before I have to kill someone."

What she didn't voice was the violent rush of fear twisting her guts, the unshakable sense of dread locking her lungs until all she could feel was the severe beat of her heart drumming at the base of her throat.

A vampire. Because she had let her instincts and emotions take over, she was now a bloodsucker who would soon need to drink. Rogan had warned her it would come to this. He wouldn't have acted without her consent, but she had asked for his bite. Hell, she had almost pleaded. She alone had made the decision and would now have to deal with it.

Somehow shackling her panic to a metal ring in the back of her mind, she watched Rogan nod. When he looked at her again, he lightly stroked the palm of her hand with his fingers.

"If the need to feed gets too strong, do what you must. Remember, you aren't human anymore."

Focusing on the tender motion of his fingers, Liv suppressed a snigger. He might be right, but she had been solely human up to now and lifelong habits had the annoying tendency to stick in mind. She wasn't yet prepared to snack off people and envision murder as her new spare-time activity.

"Don't worry, Rogan, I'll manage until you come back. What are you going to do in the meantime?"

"I'm going back to my world, see if I can call a halt to the search and get them off your back. I need to talk to the council."

"What if they have you arrested?"

A thin smile stretched his lips. Letting go of her hand, he placed a finger across her lips.

"Hush, my sweet! The only person you have to think of now is you. Keep yourself safe for twenty-four hours, and wait for me. Lie low, avoid people, but most of all stay out of the sun!"

She blinked three times before his words of caution registered. The sun! Fearful of Rogan's imminent departure and of her new condition, Liv hadn't given any thought to the brilliant star that provided life to all creatures on Earth — except vampires. No more lazy afternoons on the beach for her. No more sipping cool drinks by the pool with a bunch of friends. Bye-bye daylight, hello gloom and darkness. Forever.

Swallowing the lump in her throat, Liv forced out a smile. She'd be damned if she was going to let him see her sudden discomposure. What with Khord and a team of trackers hot on his heels, Rogan had enough on his plate. He certainly didn't need a helpless, terrorised newborn vampire into the bargain. She must be strong for him now. She would be strong.

"I know. I'll be careful."

"Go now. Dawn is on its way."

He kissed her one more time before she got into the car. When she had inserted her key into the ignition, she saw him reach for the special watch on his wrist. Then he just disappeared.

Liv stared at the empty spot where Rogan had stood. Lit by the full moon, it only showed dust and footprints. In the oppressive hours before daylight, she was alone. Alone and scared. What should she do? Where to go now that she had become a mortal danger to people? Gripping the steering wheel, she drove out of the parking lot.

An hour later and forty miles farther along the interstate highway, she had discarded all thoughts of finding a cave buried in the mountains, a hidey-hole in the heart of the forest, or a refuge far away from civilisation. The sky had migrated from black to dark blue, a pinkish line streaking her horizon.

She checked into a dingy motel. Beside hers, a single car was parked by the front entrance. With any luck the vehicle belonged to the owner, which meant she wouldn't find many people around. Perfect! Although she didn't yet feel any compulsion to bite, she couldn't trust herself. After all, this was her first shot at being a vampire.

Half asleep on duty, the clerk didn't raise an eyebrow when Liv required a room at the back of the building. He appeared bored, tired, and more than willing to get rid of her, which suited her just fine. In a way the clerk looked just like this third-rate motel—

cheap and dirty. Recalling spy movies, she parked the car right in front of her room. As unrealistic as it sounded, she might have to leave this newfound haven in a hurry. Who knew what tomorrow would bring?

Once safe in a depressingly drab bedroom, she realised she'd have to sleep with her clothes on. Although her first move was to discard her rumpled clothes, she didn't have this luxury. Her belongings at this point consisted of her handbag and car. Had circumstances been different she'd have gone to the store in the morning to purchase a pair of jeans and clean underwear. Out of the question now, for how did a vampire move along streets flooded with sunshine?

No energy to ponder yet another problem, Liv switched on the lights in the bathroom and pushed the thought to the back of her mind. She stood in front of the mirror for a while, her gaze drawn to the fang marks on the side of her neck. Two small red holes that had punctured her skin, reminders of the passionate way Rogan had made love to her. She probably should have worried about being unable to treat the deep wounds, yet there would be no infection of any kind. She wasn't human anymore.

Still unwilling to process the dreary thought, Liv let exhaustion catch up with her as the lighting fixture above her head began to blink. Eyelids heavy, she still had the presence of mind to draw the curtains shut in the bedroom. She wasn't about to disregard Rogan's warning this time.

Outside an eastern glow already brightened the sky, and rays of sunshine would hit the window soon enough. As she came closer to the bed, she swatted a bug on the nightstand. Oh, God, and she had to sleep in this foul place! Yet there was nothing she could do but grin and bear it.

Sleep called her. In spite of her weariness, Liv took a moment to stash her bag and jacket on the chair closer to the door in case she had to take off in a rush. Definitely too fond of spy movies! As she lay down on the none too clean bed, she thought she heard a soft, scratchy noise coming from the corner of the room. A good secret agent would have jumped to his feet to investigate the scraping. Instead she let sleep claim her.

Against all odds, Liv felt good when she woke up. Good, and ravenous! As much as she wanted to linger, the full meaning of her sharp hunger jerked her out of bed. She needed to feed. She wouldn't feed.

She had pulled the drapes so tight last night that a deep gloom still ruled the place. Prompted by instinct, she put her shoes on, and carried her handbag to the bathroom. In the mirror, her reflection told her the transformation into a vampire hadn't yet begun. Scary as it was, something else grabbed her attention. Her neck!

Only two barely visible scars remained right where Rogan's fangs had sunk in. Eyes widening, Liv held her breath as she prodded her throat with a cautious finger. Apart from a tiny dimple, her skin felt as soft as ever and completely healed. No pain there, no wound.

Almost transfixed, she gazed at her neck. Seconds ticked away, suddenly broken by a recurrent sound — the scratchy noise she had heard before falling asleep. Irritated by this insistent grating Liv turned around. At the door, she peered into the bedroom. She spotted it at once, and all coherent thoughts fled like a flock of hunted birds.

Her mind ablaze with panic, she bolted towards the exit, threw the door wide open, and burst out into the sunlight.

Chapter Thirteen

Instantly struck by hot, golden rays, Liv froze. Her mind went blank, and for a minute she couldn't remember the reason she wasn't supposed to stand outside. Heart pounding, eyes riveted to the bedroom door, she willed herself to cool down, to recapture a semblance of rationality. But the sight of the monster inside was branded in her mind, and the simple act of breathing had mutated into an insuperable obstacle.

Bathed in mid-afternoon summer sunshine, Liv began to sweat. Poised to flee, still looking at the door, her panic attack on the verge of wearing off, she kept on drawing air in and out of her lungs. Nothing moved. Finally the silence surrounding the motel reminded her of the current situation, and she felt a wild urge to run to cover. Too late, though!

Freaked out by the mouse, rat, or whatever gigantic rodent was in there, she had been standing in the sun for at least a minute. How long did it take to fry up on the spot? How long could a vampire withstand such a treatment before bursting into flames?

Liv licked her dry lips. Startled by this new development, she raised her head to squint at the fiery ball glowing bright in a cloudless sky. Stretching her arms out, she offered herself to the hot caress, taking new pleasure in the warming sensation that should have been forbidden to her.

As wonderful as the sun on her skin felt, she had other fish to fry — number one being the huge rodent in the room. Holy mackerel, she had slept right beside the hateful creature for hours! Could life get any grosser?

As though basking in sunshine gave her unexpected strength, Liv made her mind up. Her first act as a non-burning vampire would be to overcome her fear by dealing with the hairy monster. Resolve hardening her muscles, she took the few steps separating her from the entrance.

The room hadn't been pitch-dark in the first place, but with the door wide open Liv easily saw the grungy contents — the unmade bed, the stained carpet, the chair where she had left her jacket, the lit bathroom to her left, and, in the farthest corner, watching her, the rat.

Gooseflesh rising over the surface of her body, her determination melting like heated wax, Liv didn't stop to think. She rushed to the chair, grabbed her jacket, retreated to the bathroom in the face of her enemy, retrieved her bag with shaky hands, and got the hell out of the motel where Alfred Hitchcock had no doubt shot *Psycho*.

So much for overcoming her phobia. Disappointing, yes, but she figured a non-burning vampire couldn't be expected to act as ruthlessly as a true vampire. With this questionable excuse in mind, she hurried to her car. As her tyres screeched on the gravelly driveway, she turned right onto the main road.

Mindful of the speed limit, Liv reached the outskirts of the small town of Bentham by late afternoon. Hungry, thirsty, and needing time to ponder recent events, she pulled over by a strip mall.

She strode to the nearest restaurant, bag in hand. Four or five tables had been set out front for patrons to enjoy the warm weather — no way would she pass on this golden opportunity. Without a single glance around, she wolfed down three cheese and ham sandwiches, a plate of home-made chips, two big chocolate cookies, and a glass of orange juice.

The sense of relief that washed over her when she pushed her plate back had her grinning. She was able to sit in the sun, see her reflection in the restaurant window, and look at shoppers like they were people, not bloody food on legs. Without stretching it too far, she felt positive she could chew mountains of garlic. What a glorious day!

But how? Rogan might know the answer. He had only been gone for a few hours, yet the vacant spot in her heart had his name on it. What was he doing? Would he ever come back to her?

A stray dog came sniffing around, its tongue lolling, its brown eyes holding hope of a different kind. When Liv offered it the last fries, the dog licked its chops before grabbing the chips with great care. Then it padded away, tail wagging, on the lookout for a new adventure.

Unlike her new furry friend, Liv sought quiet and peace. The past forty-eight hours had been a whirling mass sucking her in, a complicated vortex she had fallen into willingly. She could have ditched Rogan and his vampire universe anytime, but she hadn't.

Instead she'd seen to it that Khord's silver bullet didn't kill him. What was more, when she'd tried her so-called power on the warrior in the warehouse it hadn't affected him in the least. Come to think of it, she might well have treated him for smallpox.

Regarding vampires, she really did have a healing power. So why did they believe her a deadly threat to their race? Why did their legend mention her as a Bringer of Death? Whoever came up with that myth must have been loaded, stuffed full with human blood. Did they use drugs over there? Could their prophecy writer have been hallucinating at the time?

Liv smiled at her reflection in the window. Making fun of vampires felt good right now—a pity she must get a move on. The sun had already dipped to the west, tree shadows lengthened across the parking lot, shoppers left the mall. Time to hide from bloody creatures of the night. Time to get ready for whatever fate had in store for her.

She bought a new pair of jeans, a skirt, tops, shoes, underwear, and a toiletries bag inside the mall. While she was there she asked for directions to the nearest clean motel. She must have put too much emphasis on the word 'clean' because the young shop assistant at the till nodded vigorously. Better he looked at her in a funny way than facing another monster rodent.

She saw the motel in question, a mile down the road. Night had fallen anyway and she wouldn't have missed the blinking, flashy red and yellow lights indicating the entrance. From the outside the building looked recent. Indoors it matched her expectations.

Fresh linen on the bed, immaculate towels, polished furniture—the room even smelt flowery. And once she had switched all the lights on to dispel the darkness—*oh goody, the age of miracles isn't past*—no bugs crawling on the nightstand, no beady-eyed rats about to pounce on her.

The bathroom featured a white, spotless sink, white tiles on the walls, and an oblong-shaped hairdryer. After she had brushed her teeth, Liv felt compelled to check her canines. They looked like they always had, and felt no sharper. Then she stripped before stepping into the shower. Temperature as hot as she could take it, she let invigorating water glide down her body.

Enjoying this soothing feeling she wondered about her next step. Rogan had been certain he'd find her anywhere. He had told her to stay put and wait for him. As she hadn't come up with a better plan that was exactly what she'd do. Work worried her, though. She'd call in sick first thing tomorrow morning. Mondays were usually busy at the office, but they'd do fine without her.

Turning the water off, Liv stepped out of the shower, marvelling at the fact that she hadn't appreciated the beneficial effects of a good shower in a long time — of simply taking time to take care of herself. One should definitely pay more attention to mundane comforts.

She dried off before wrapping herself up in a bath towel. Holding the hairdryer like a gun she let warm air blow away the last remnants of her night in that dingy, sordid motel. She experienced a wonderful sensation of cleanliness as if she had got over the weird, incredible events of the past two days. Once fresh and dry, she walked out of the bathroom.

"I thought you'd never come out of there!"

Chapter Fourteen

Heart pumping several delicious beats at the reassuring sound of his voice, she ran into his open arms.

"Rogan!"

She felt the hard bulge in his jeans when he hugged her tightly. Desire instantly stung her whole body, halting her breathing, pushing her to stare into his golden eyes. She saw the same desire there, saw that he would take her before anything else.

Amazed at the force of the attraction drawing her to Rogan, Liv rose on tiptoes to kiss him. After all she had been through, the sight of his full lips almost felt too much to bear. She needed his mouth crushing hers. She had to have his tongue caressing and suckling hers.

But, before she could reach that tantalising mouth, he let go of her and took a step back. Startled, she listened to the harsh rhythm of her own breathing, felt the hungry moistness leaking between her legs.

Looking at her neckline he pulled hard on the towel, and flung it away. A brief light glittered in his gaze as he watched her naked limbs. Under his intense scrutiny a tinge of heat inflamed her cheeks, only to burn stronger when he touched her breasts.

He tweaked her nipples and she sighed, his abrupt stroke discharging jolts of pleasure throughout her body. Her pulse quickening at his unexpected brusqueness, she let his name pass her lips.

"Rogan."

He didn't let her say more. He grabbed her hips, turned her round, and pushed her onto the bed. She landed on all fours, her skin puckered with the same violent desire he had for her.

No foreplay this time. Not a single moment devoted to tenderness because he was about to take her like an animal. *Yes. Oh, dear God, yes.* Knees and hands bearing her weight and position, mind ablaze with urgency, she imagined what he must be seeing.

The length of her back stiff with anticipation, the fullness of her ass, the split between her buttocks exposed to his hungry gaze, the wetness coming out of her. As if the thought acted like a trigger, a new rush of desire streaked her stomach and she crumpled the bed sheet in her fingers.

She faced the opposite wall and heard the unmistakable sound of a zip, felt the coarse texture of his jeans against her thighs. Would he take his pants off or just drop them down like a man unable to stall his sexual urges? Tilting her head to catch a glimpse of him, his imperious order halted her.

"Don't move!"

His harsh injunction increased her lust. She thought her blood was jumping out of her veins. She thought her sex was stretching towards his, reaching for his vampire maleness. She didn't move. Mouth dry, she had to close her eyes to refrain from moaning.

"You're so exciting."

She didn't move, but she bit her lower lip, keeping a cry inside. He raked his nails on the fullness of her buttocks. A whimper escaped her, and she jerked forward.

"I said don't move!"

Her breasts felt heavy enough to bring her down, her belly streaked with want. His tip touched her slit, swiftly baring her wet hole. She forced herself to keep still, her instincts screaming with longing. Because she faced the bedroom wall, she pictured Rogan's hand around his cock, aiming, splitting her inner lips open to grant himself passage.

He gripped her thighs. His strong fingers kneading her flesh, he embedded his dick into her. Her uncontrolled wail seemed to jar his deepest instincts. As harsh as a creature of the night devoid of human emotions, he pounded her. The louder she moaned the harder he penetrated her. Each of his vigorous, persistent thrusts felt like a bar of pleasure driving her towards ecstasy.

He wasn't making any noise, yet she knew he was loving it. She felt it in her bones. His hands tensed around her thighs from the enjoyment he was giving her and taking out of her. He had wanted her in this carnal position. He had felt the domineering need to possess her like a wolf in heat.

His bestial instincts had taken over. His repeated hits took her breath away, prompting her to lower her head onto the bedspread. She raised her buttocks, and he grunted. She opened up to him completely, and he implanted his cock in her even deeper.

Her sharp cry of unruly satisfaction seemed to let off the true vampire in him. Grasping her hips, yanking her back with every strike of his dick, he banged her time and time again. Her insides on fire, her mind reduced to a bottomless void of pleasure, she bit into the bedspread to stifle the shrieks welling up in her.

He was bringing her to climax so hard she thought she might lose a piece of her humanity. She didn't feel like a woman anymore, but like an untamed bitch mating for life, a savage she-wolf submitting to the power of the leader of the pack. And she loved it.

She loved the wild vampiric instincts she had brought out in him, the rough pressure of his fingers latched on her waist, the hammering of his engorged cock digging into her.

Somehow she needed what he craved. Once more she forgot all about his poisonous fangs capable of turning her into a vampire. Nothing felt real but the urge to be marked as his, the desperate pull to come while he broke her skin and drank her vital substance. Flipping her hair to the side, she raised her head and bared her neck for him.

"Bite me. Now!"

Totally attuned to her, he bent over to slide his fingers under her shoulders. Still buried in her, he drew her up. Her back pressed against his chest, she began to pant and sob when he cupped her breasts and his thrusts became short and rapid.

She wanted to feel his sharp teeth on her skin. She wanted to feel the biting pain where his fangs pierced her flesh. She couldn't. As she sensed his mouth coming down on her neck, a gigantic orgasm rocked her out of reality. She came furiously, registering from far away his own grunts of pleasure, and the violent tremors shaking his body.

Deprived of strength, breathless, Liv sank onto the bed. Rogan let her slide before flipping a side of the bedspread over her naked body. Although she already missed his hands on her, she felt complete. He had so fully satisfied her she wondered how such a magnificent sensation could be real. Lids half-closed, she relished this unforgettable moment.

Then a brief noise confirmed their wild lovemaking had been no dream, a zipping sound terminating an unbelievable experience. In a way, she could have cried from joy.

As she turned her head towards where Rogan stood, a light jab reminded her she had been bitten for the second time. She sat up to touch the soft spot on the side of her neck. Two pearls of blood showed on her finger when she looked at it. She licked the bright red liquid, her blood, her vital link to the vampire-man looming over her.

She glanced up to meet his eyes, still focused on her neck. The intensity of his gaze made her shiver, annihilating any sensation of wellbeing. Suddenly she felt cold, and wrapped the bedspread tighter around her body. Rogan opened his mouth to speak, but a knock on the door halted him. Whatever he had been about to say turned into some kind of irritated bark.

"What?"

As the door opened, Liv wondered if Rogan had been expecting someone. Had he found some help? Of course not—help never came when needed. On the other hand, she had trouble picturing Rogan asking for room service. He was more the break-and-enter type. So, when Khord came into the bedroom, she felt completely at a loss.

No, no, no, not now! Not him!

Adrenaline awakening all her senses, strangled with fear, Liv braced herself for the inevitable fight to come. Except that Rogan remained motionless while Khord stepped up to him, a look of reverence stiffening his ugly features. He stopped just short of Rogan, and bowed to him while holding out a black shape she couldn't quite make out.

Holy mackerel, what was going on here? Had they both been brainwashed in the past twelve hours? Had she inexplicably fallen into the fourth dimension? Unable to figure out the weird scene she witnessed, Liv gaped at Rogan. For a second, it felt like observing a total stranger. Or someone she might have come across in the street, but not let him touch her. Mind blank, guts twisted with dread, all she could do was whisper his name.

"Rogan..."

He slowly turned his handsome face towards her. So slowly her heart missed a beat. His sudden sneer made her blood race, causing her to tighten the bedspread around her shoulders.

Feeling trapped like a frightened mouse, she couldn't help but goggle at the malice in his eyes, seeming to take a wicked pleasure in her obvious confusion. Then his mouth puckered, and her disarray turned to downright fear as he uttered three ghastly words.

"Guess again, baby!"

Chapter Fifteen

What the hell did he mean by that? Why was he looking at her with such a mocking, satisfied grin? Surely he'd reach down in a second, swoop her in his arms and tell her to wake up. It was just a bad dream, an awful, gut-wrenching nightmare and everything would be all right.

But he didn't. Instead he stretched his lips into a scorn, and his hurtful words shattered her soul.

"Oh, my, aren't you a delightful piece of meat."

Her legs weighed a ton. Inner spasms twitched her nerve endings. Her stomach dropped down, at the same time trying to push her last meal back up. She swallowed to bring the fries and sandwiches under control, yet the horrible sensation didn't fade. And when Khord sniggered loudly her cheeks and forehead began to burn.

Naked. Helpless on a bed. Trapped in a motel room with two ferocious vampires, one of whom hated her. The other... Well, the other had just made love to her and was now treating her like a cow he had milked.

To top it all, the brute's idiotic snigger grated on her nerves.

"Enough!"

Rogan's order shut him up immediately. Before Liv's astonished gaze, Khord went down on one knee, head bowed.

"Forgive me, my king."

"Wait for me outside."

Dismissed, the brute stood up. Without a single glance at her, he strode out of the room. Liv stared at the closed door, realising they were alone. She was incapable of looking at Rogan.

"Get dressed."

In a way, his command should've been considered good news. If this Rogan-thing wanted her dressed, he had no intention of killing her right now. Yet she was so aware of his towering presence, so tied to the intimacy they had shared that she felt unable to move.

Did he perceive her shock? Did he sense she wasn't a computer to process data at lightning speed? Whatever the case, he walked to the table where she had left her recent purchases, rummaged through the bigger bag, and threw a bunch of clothes onto the bed.

"There. Now, get dressed."

This vampire wouldn't tolerate denial. In spite of her total dismay, Liv could see he was used to being obeyed. Although she looked at him long and hard, her mind only told her the vampire in front of her was Rogan. Same face, same golden-freckled eyes, same voice.

Had he been human she might have figured he had a twin brother, but vampires had no kin. Fully aware of the big risk she was about to take, she called him by the name she wanted to be true.

"Rogan."

This time, his look of genuine surprise didn't reassure her in the least. When he spoke, the full power of his words hit her.

"I thought you'd have been smarter. How long is it going to take you to understand? I am not Rogan."

"Well, who are you then?"

"My name is Raskhan. I'm the king of the Overworld."

Shit, oh shit. What was she supposed to do with that? Nothing yet. He snapped his fingers towards the foot of the bed where her clothes lay. Yes, he wanted her to get dressed, she got that!

"Where's Rogan?"

"Precisely where he should be."

Bedspread tight around her shoulders, Liv crept forward on her butt to sit on the edge. Collecting her stuff she stood up. Only then did she realise the cover clinging to her skin was attached to the bottom corners of the bed — firmly attached.

Either she let it drop or she made a run for the bathroom. In both cases he'd see her naked. The prospect of him eyeing her bare body had lost any appeal, so she tried to voice her demand in a firm voice.

"Would you mind?"

With a half-smile he had been watching her making a fool of herself. As she spoke he crossed his arms over his chest, clearly showing his refusal to avert his gaze. Although he knew her body inside and out, it was obvious he had no intention of missing a free striptease show.

"I would."

Right. No luck there. Let's try something else. She would not run to the bathroom. She would not give him the satisfaction of feeling ashamed. In a manner Liv hoped was queenly, she'd slowly walk to the bathroom. Holding her clothes with one hand, she let go of the bedspread. Without glancing at the spitting image of Rogan she took a step forward. Then a second, a third, her back so straight she could have passed for an automaton.

As she extended her hand to seize the handle, a weight in her back forced her to flatten against the door. Startled, she dropped her clothes, her hands instinctively rushing up to cushion the impact. Left cheek pressed hard against the door, cold wood grazing her nipples and belly, legs slightly open to keep her balance, the zip of his jeans moulded into her lower back, she dared not utter a single sound, dared not attempt a single move.

"Watch your steps, little girl. If you misbehave, I intend to make you pay for it."

Although Liv wasn't sure what he was referring to, she recognised the ring of truth in his tone. Fear felt like a lifelong companion by now, but to her utter disbelief something else ran far stronger in her veins.

How could her body betray her so? How could she feel aroused by a barbarian pinning her to a door? Yet she did, her stomach curling with temptation, her heart pulsing with desire. Restraint foremost in her mind, determined to conceal her emotion, Liv played along with him.

"And if I behave?"

He touched the sides of her breasts. With a lazy downward motion, he caressed her ribs, her hips, her thighs. Eyes squeezed shut, she mustered all her self-control to refrain from shivering. When his mouth brushed against her ear, she almost gasped.

"I might keep you for myself."

Arrogant and conceited, that was what he was! If watching Khord act like a slave around him hadn't convinced her, this simple sentence did. King or not, he was nothing like Rogan.

"What makes you think I want to be yours?"

"You already are."

He knew. Although full of himself and insensitive he had perceived her lust for him. But she'd rather pass for an idiot than admit it. Besides he deserved to be put in his place.

"You're wrong!"

"Am I? Really?"

Moving back, he gave her an inch to breathe easier. The pressure of his jeans on her back vanished, but he seized her neck with one hand to keep her face pressed to the cool door.

"Come on, little girl, tell me you don't crave my cock. Say it, I want to hear you say it!"

"I don't…"

He trapped the words in her throat with his finger. Tracing a line down the small of her back, he slid it between her buttocks. Already reaching her opening, he wove his way home to glide into her wetness.

Taken aback, Liv let out a deep sigh. Nipples erect and rubbing against the door, she closed her eyes to focus on a way to stop him, to cool the heatwave demanding possession of her body. Very close to her ear, harsh and obnoxious, Raskhan provoked her.

"Do you still not want my cock?"

He inserted his finger into her sex. She drew in a sharp breath. Up and down he rubbed her flesh with quick, arousing motions.

"How do you like this, kitten? It feels good, doesn't it? Oh yeah, so good! You didn't get that with Rogan, did you?"

Her mind rebelled at the thought of deceiving Rogan, yet her cunt couldn't help sucking in the damn digit. Torn between heart and flesh, she managed to bawl him out.

"Don't you dare mention his name!"

Out of the blue, he retrieved his finger. The sudden emptiness in her brought such a longing she felt like crying out from frustration. But Raskhan wasn't done with her as he kept her pressed against the door.

"Aren't you a brave little fighter? Such a pity you're lying to yourself."

"I'm not lying. I'm in love with Rogan and you're just... You're just a..."

Her voice trailed off. Unable to find the right words to shut him up, she wished her sex would stop throbbing.

"A what? Open your eyes, kitten. It seems to me your love serves different masters."

Now this was too much to bear. She had to do something to end this ridiculous scene. Her strength being no match against his, maybe she could pretend to pass out. Would he swallow it? As Liv took a second to think it through, he placed his thumb on her clitoris.

"Now we're gonna see who's right."

Chapter Sixteen

Did the room lurch forward when he touched her? Not quite believable. Did her mind and body reel with the motions he submitted her to? *Oh yes, oh yes, oh yes!* Taking his time to draw short circles on her clit with his finger, he licked the blood oozing from the bite he had inflicted on her. She jerked, her instinctive reaction causing her nipples to rub against the bathroom door. She was at his mercy and, holy mackerel, she delighted in it.

Without warning, he inserted his tongue in her ear, and the speed of his hand changed. Alternating between quick and slow, he knew how to use his digit to send jolts of pleasure throughout her body. Flat on the door, framing her face, her hands seemed to take on a life of their own. They balled into fists, knuckles rapping against the wood.

He couldn't not see the effect he had on her. His tongue licking her ear, he couldn't not notice the tremors shaking her body, the sudden harshness of her breathing, or the insane heat coming off her sex.

Then he ceased its rapturous motions, and he whispered in her ear.

"You horny bitch! Rogan can go back where he came from because I'm the best fuck you've ever had."

Although his soft-spoken words hit her hard, she craved his touch. She hadn't been aware a single digit could create such teeth-clenching joy. When he began tapping her erect flesh with his thumb, she whimpered. But her unchecked moans didn't blank out his spiteful whispers.

"Don't ever pretend otherwise!"

The beat of his finger on her pulsating clit brought a tear of pleasure to her eye. She hated him for the way he was treating her, she hated herself for wanting more and more. In the pit of her stomach, she felt the rise of a familiar sensation built up by his relentless touch.

"One more thing, little girl." As if he needed her full attention, he quit tapping to knead her open wet slit with the palm of his hand. "I can make you come any time I want."

With that, he retrieved his hand, and pinched her buttock hard enough to make her wince. Then he let go of her. Free, brutally torn out of the bliss she had been basking in, her legs buckled. Like a marionette discarded by its puppeteer, she crumpled to the floor. Breathing in fits and starts, fighting off the imperious need to touch herself in front of him, she raised her head to find out he was already at the bedroom door.

Her Rogan would never stare the way Raskhan was gloating over her now. His eyes shining with self-satisfaction and malice, his lips twisted in a sneer, he pointed a mocking finger at her.

"Before long you'll be begging me to suck your cunt."

A blur of colour, and he was gone. The bedroom door clicked, silence following his departure. Liv figured he wouldn't allow her to spend the entire day on the floor, but she took a minute to attempt to gather her scattered thoughts. God, how she hated that guy!

Hands flat on the wall, she had to use it like a prop to stand up. Still panting with frustration, she got dressed. As she zipped up her jeans, her eyes fell on a bright red ashtray lying on the table. Before she realised the consequences of her gesture, she hurled it against the opposite wall. She might not have possessed a full vampire's strength, yet the fragile object smashed the wall with a resonant bang.

The bedroom door burst open. A single glance at the ashtray on the floor told Raskhan everything he needed to know. Still smirking, he strode up to her, his body seeming to take up the whole room. Raising both hands to ward him off, Liv took a step back.

"Don't touch me!"

The powerful vampire didn't touch her. A sly smile attached to his lips, he handed her the black thing Khord had given him earlier — a watch. The same kind of watch the warrior in the warehouse had tried to clasp around her wrist — a device to cross between worlds.

The king wanted to take her with him. With Rogan gone, how would she survive in an unknown universe filled with bloodsuckers? Would he look for her over there? In desperate need of a strong drink to steady her nerves, Liv stared at the watch and shook her head.

"Don't even think about it, I'm not coming with you."

"Oh yes, you are."

She kept on shaking her head, all the while watching his mirthful gaze, his beautiful features reflecting his wily amusement.

"Either you put it on, or I'll make you. What's it gonna be, kitten?"

Careful to avoid the contact of his fingers, she took the watch and fastened it around her wrist. She was going to the Overworld, to the place where only vampires dwelt. No humans there. No help for her.

"How did you find me?"

When Raskhan didn't answer, Liv dropped the subject. Vaguely conscious that he was packing all her stuff, she almost cringed at the fleeting thoughts crossing her mind. Would she see her parents again? Her sister? Who would cover for her at work? Had she locked her front door? Was she going to become a missing person, an anonymous face on a precinct wall? Where was her car parked? Oh, she missed Rogan so much!

She drew in a long breath to settle the drumming of her heart. As Raskhan jabbed his chin out, she lifted her arm up. He pressed a button on the watch, and she closed her eyes.

She reckoned she heard a weird whooshing sound, then her stomach lurched briefly. The sensation was over in a second, even before she opened her eyes to take a look around her. In all likelihood the trip to the Overworld was already over. Now that was what she called a quick jump.

White. Marble. Cold. And so bright.

The vast room looked like a temple. Maybe a Greek entrance hall of some sort. Tall white columns seemed to bear the weight of the whole building and reached up to an overhead dome.

Covering the points of the compass, four wide marble staircases led up to open galleries all around, supported by white arches on the inner side. In every nook and corner, life-sized statues faced the centre of the hall with blind eyes. But something else deserved careful attention—no windows, no apparent door leading outside.

As she slowly spun around, Liv instantly thought of ancient gods, of grand palaces erected for Zeus and his divine retinue. The place was stunning, if not the last thing she had expected. Impressive, magnificent, it also gave off an air of arctic, rigid grandeur. Surprisingly enough, she didn't feel cold. She had trouble steadying her rapid heartbeat, but she didn't feel cold.

"Welcome to my kingdom."

Ignoring his boisterous tone and her awe of this sumptuous place, Liv studied the quiet flurry of activity around them. Dressed in long, flowing black robes, vampires came and went, carrying things, going places. Servants? Helpers? In any case, they appeared human.

Although they all bowed to Raskhan as they passed by, she noticed an odd look on their faces when their eyes fell on her. If she hadn't known better, she'd have bet they were wary of her. But why? Because of that Bringer of Death crap? Did they also think she had something to do with their ancient legend? Were they all that gullible?

She felt as if someone was watching her. She glanced up to the long gallery. A vampire stood motionless at the top of one of the staircases, observing her. About fifty or sixty years old, a mass of silver hair framing deep-set blue eyes and a hooked nose, he didn't seem wary of her. More like intrigued. For a wonder, this one didn't look scary.

Before she could give it more thought, Raskhan unfastened the watch from her wrist and snapped his fingers. One of the servants rushed to him, face expectant. The king quickly handed him her bag, then seized Liv's arm to push her towards the young vampire.

"Take her upstairs!"

Swept along, she nearly stumbled into the arms of the servant. But, as she caught her balance, the automatic shrinking of the young vampire didn't escape her. Like a reflex, he backed away from her. Then he got a grip on himself, and indicated the opposite staircase.

"This way."

Always keeping his distance, he led her up to the first floor, past windowless yet brightly lit galleries, and along a splendid hallway. Only when he stopped in front of an ornamented oak door with markings did Liv realise the walls, ceiling and floor emitted light. *How did they do that?*

As soon as he had pushed open the heavy door and thrust the bag in her hands, the servant took a brisk step back to let her in. Although he seemed a young, strong vampire, he shrank from her. How ironic!

Left alone, she looked around. Her first impression was of a marble bedroom for a monk — or a cell. After all, it wasn't as if she was an honoured guest from another kingdom. More like a prisoner.

No windows, but the lighting fixture aroused her interest. As she applied her hand on the nearest wall it felt warm to the touch, and a diffuse white glow enveloped her spread fingers. *Very neat!*

Discovering this new place allowed her to forget about where she was. Later she'd think of a plan to escape, or at least to stay alive until Rogan came for her. Because he had to. Because he wouldn't abandon her at the hands of a cruel, infuriating king.

She sat on the mattress, firm but comfortable. The leather armchair offered another cosy haven. When she slumped onto it, Liv noticed some kind of wooden closet on the other side of the door. Quick on her feet, she pulled on the handle, but in spite of her efforts the panel remained locked. Too bad! Now she'd have to fall back on the hundreds of books displayed to find a clue as to the reason of her presence here.

First, she went to the writing desk, and pulled open both drawers. Pencils, an eraser, a sharpener, some Scotch tape, graphics, and dozens of sheets filled with numbers sat in the right drawer. Nothing interesting there. Then she pulled a very big, heavy book from the left drawer. Using both hands, she placed it carefully on the writing desk. Bound with worn-out leather, it looked more like an ancient manuscript than a novel.

As Liv lifted open the front cover, she felt like a trespasser. How weird was that? Whoever wrote this book must have been a lengthy storyteller, she'd need weeks to read it through. As it happened, she didn't believe she had weeks — probably not even days.

She flipped through the pages, dipping into passages, overlooking entire sections written in a foreign language and impossible to decipher, reading selectively until a particular turn of phrase caught her eye. There, spelt in black letters — *The Bringer of Death.*

Liv realised she was holding the book of prophecies Rogan had told her about. No wonder it looked so ancient. Should she marvel at this stroke of luck? Or wonder if someone had deliberately left it there for her to find? Now, who would do that and why? Holy mackerel, but she didn't care a whit about the reason for the manuscript's presence. She must read this!

As she bent over the book, her heart suddenly veered. Something rattled in the pit of her stomach. A mix of excitement and apprehension, the uncanny sensation raised goose pimples on her arms and grew stronger with each passing second. Acting on impulse, Liv put the book back in the drawer. She stood up, a hand fluttering to her belly to soothe the baffling gut reaction she was experiencing. When her cell door banged open, she stared with wide eyes.

Chapter Seventeen

This could not be happening. Dear God, why him? Now that his eyes bore into her, she recognised the inescapable feeling for what it was—desire and anticipation. She had felt him coming, no doubt about that.

Her body had responded to his. Like a sexual connection. Like an inner vibe beyond her control. Truth be told, she had felt the same vibe in the motel room. As she had run into his arms, believing he was Rogan, she had sensed something similar then. And she had dismissed it. But no, no, no, this could not be happening.

She hated his guts. She loathed the fact that he played vampire almighty and toyed with her weaknesses. She couldn't stand his arrogance, meanness, and superiority. Most of all, she despised herself for desiring him, for wanting to feel his finger on her again.

He had used her feelings for Rogan to jump her bones, he had taken her prisoner into a blood-sucking alien world, and he was probably plotting another of his devious schemes. Yet when she looked at his gorgeous face, she wanted to shiver and spread her legs.

Why had Rogan left her? Where was he? How come she wasn't connected to him instead of the vampire king now stepping into her cell? If destiny had decided to play a trick on her, it wasn't funny. So Liv conjured an image of Rogan to muster up her strength before Raskhan could lay down his cards.

"Where's Rogan?"

"Hopefully dead."

'Hopefully' meant that he had no clue as to Rogan's whereabouts. Her saviour must be alive somewhere, biding his time to rescue her, surely drawing a cunning scheme to free her.

"Why do you hate him so much? What has he done to you?"

"None of your business. Here, wear this!"

Raskhan threw a light bundle at her. She caught it with one hand, recognising at once a similar black robe to the ones the vampires wore. Was she supposed to blend in the landscape? As if that would happen with bloodsuckers wary of her every movement.

"Why?"

"You're to stand before the council."

Liv swallowed, a knot of fear obstructing her throat. Whatever they wanted with her, it couldn't be good.

"And if I don't want to?"

"I think we've already covered that."

His mischievous smile reminded her of their first encounter. The way Raskhan had pounded her body until she exploded with passion, the way she had betrayed Rogan. But she didn't have the will and the energy to dwell on that now. Too painful. Too confusing.

"What if you can't force me? What if I'm stronger than you?"

He regarded her as if she had just lost her marbles. Great. On top of stupid she had just managed to pass for a whacko. As he took a step towards her, she tensed but stood her ground.

"What if I'm a vampire?"

He burst out laughing. Captive of his merriment, his features softened. Dear God, he was so attractive!

"You aren't a vampire. Where did you get this foolish idea?"

This time, his assertion surprised her. Sure, she had been able to withstand the full power of the sun today, but for how long? Her transformation had to come at some point.

"Because Rogan bit me, and he said I was a vampire now."

"Well, Rogan was wrong, wasn't he?"

As soon as the question left his lips, his mood changed. Not teasing anymore, his gaze showed irritation.

"And is that all you can think of? I'm sick and tired of hearing Rogan's praise. I don't think I can stand you whining about him one more minute. The man is gone, deal with it!"

His eyes darker than a midnight storm, he had never looked so powerful.

Dumbfounded, she stared at him. "Are you jealous?"

He licked his lips, his sensual gesture calling to mind a male wolf dominating his female.

"No reason to be. You're mine now."

Despite her precarious situation in this unknown world, the simple words stabbed her and a deep coldness suddenly iced her veins.

"You may well be able to satisfy my body, but don't be mistaken, you will never touch my heart. Never."

She didn't see him move. Yet he was behind her, his marble chest pressed against her back, his hands on her breasts. She gasped. She dropped the black robe. The coldness departed in a flash, immediately replaced by a wave of heat as his palms found her nipples through the cotton halter top. His face on her neck, he passed his lips over her already healed bite mark. Slow and grazing, he licked her ear.

"Who said I wanted to touch your heart?"

He grasped her sensitive teats, and his grand palace seemed to rock beneath her. He twirled the erect flesh, and the vibe writhed in her stomach. Cheeks hot, pulse in tatters from his unexpected move, she pushed the words out of her mouth.

"You've made your point. Let go of me."

Although she couldn't see him, she knew the sly smile was back on his face. He lowered his hands to her belly, soon sliding them down to her crotch. Then he whispered in her ear.

"That's my girl!"

Before she could react, he had whizzed around her again. Holding out the robe, he shook his head and emitted a 'tsk, tsk' sound.

"Such a pity we don't have time right now!"

By now Liv knew better than to try to change his mind. She removed her clothes, keeping her underwear on. He watched each of her movements. As she lifted the robe over her head, her gaze fell on his groin. His jeans were bulging, and his hands had balled into fists.

When she looked up, she noticed the obvious tension swelling the muscles of his neck, hardening the straight line of his jaw, creasing his brow. His whole body strained, he was actually making an all-out effort to drive back his lust. For him to do that only meant he had no choice but to give her over to the council without delay.

She wouldn't be a woman if she didn't seek revenge. Aiming wrong, she let the robe down on her face. Blind, pretending to get tangled in the loose folds, she called out to him.

"Would you give me a hand?"

Seconds stretched away while her body hair rose as if a magnetic gust had invaded the room. She thought he would bail out. Then she felt two strong hands on her head actually attempting to disentangle her. Arms up, on the verge of being freed, she feigned confusion and took a step forward.

Their bodies collided. His hands froze. As if hit with a powerful blow, his chest seemed to cave in. Yet his paralysis didn't last long. Quicker than a heartbeat, he brusquely groped her buttocks. He sank his fingers into her flesh while he pressed her hard against him.

Although she had initiated this retaliation, Liv wasn't positive she'd come out the winner. Not with him. Not with something in her calling out to him. Intensely aware of his rigid body along her bare skin, still blinded by the fluid fabric, she kept as still as a cornered hostage.

"Fuck!"

His rough cry jolted her. She almost toppled over as the brick wall grasping her vanished. Silence and emptiness followed. What was he doing now? Donning the robe only took her an instant. She glanced around to find out she was alone in the cell.

Where had he gone? And, God, wasn't his damn speed irritating? Smoothing out the black clothing, Liv walked out into the hallway.

Facing the wall, hands flat on the marble surface, arms straight and head down between them, Raskhan's position reminded her of a marathon runner recovering from an all too exhausting run. Seemingly sensing her presence, he straightened up and strode towards the stairs without looking at her.

"Come!"

She had done it. Cool and composed, she had managed to drive him to intense frustration just like he had done to her in the motel room. Solely relying on her feminine assets she had contrived to put him in her shoes. Sure, it wouldn't last, but for a little while she'd enjoy her victory. Following him, she stuck out her tongue at his stiff back. Tit for tat!

Down they went, across the Greek godly entrance hallway she had landed in earlier, past the staircase where she had spotted the older vampire with grey hair, straight on to an open door. Raskhan never checked back to see if she was following him, and the servants around the place steered clear of them.

The vampire king didn't stop at the threshold. Master of the palace, he entered the room like a conqueror. Although apprehensive, Liv had no option but to tag along behind him.

The interior very much resembled a courtroom. Up on a large bench sat three vampires, their faces hostile, eyeing her from head to toe with icy stares. As Liv advanced towards them, a fourth vampire emerged from behind a statue to sit alongside her judges—the older one with grey hair. Only his eyes softened when he glanced at her.

Having walked around the bench, Raskhan pulled back the empty chair in the middle. Of course, where else would the king preside over a hearing? In front of the judges' bench, five or six feet apart stood some kind of witness stand. Looking at it, Liv figured the stand was meant for her. Swallowing a lump in her throat, she marched into battle.

As she reached the witness box, the vampire beside Raskhan unrolled a piece of paper. "Human, you have been brought before us today to answer for your actions."

"What actions?"

He furrowed his brow. No doubt piqued by her brisk tone, he glared at her. To his right Raskhan banged his fist on the table.

"You don't get to question anyone here. Watch your mouth, human!"

"Is that my new nickname? How sweet of you!"

She knew she was playing with fire, but if they had wanted her dead she'd be pushing up the daisies by now. Besides it was high time to oppose them. Without giving Raskhan any chance to vent his growing irritation, Liv addressed the vampire holding the paper.

"OK. What are the charges against me?"

"Crime of lese-majesty."

She couldn't believe her ears. They were accusing her of a crime against Raskhan. He had assaulted her, not the other way round. This was far worse than unfairness, this was utter madness.

"Do you have anything to say, human?"

Oh yes, she did. Unfortunately she didn't have time to express her righteous indignation. Raskhan banged his fist on the table again, his voice booming through the courtroom.

"No, she doesn't, and I don't have all day. Let's move on, shall we? Read her sentence."

Icy and unwavering, the judge's gaze fell on her. "You have slain the king's brother. You will be put to death."

Chapter Eighteen

That had to be the briefest trial ever. Although Liv felt positive she could have walked, two servants dragged her out of the courtroom. Her feet didn't touch the floor as they flew upstairs, along galleries, into a room where they dropped her on a metallic chair. Despite her total bafflement, she perceived their unease. They rushed her so because they couldn't wait to be rid of her.

Left alone, she took her head in her hands. She emitted a low whimper and swung her body back and forth. Her mind in unison with the gentle rocking motion, her pulse soon decreased to its regular rhythm and her thoughts clicked into place.

Holy mackerel, but they were really going to execute her for a crime she hadn't committed! Not just a random crime, but the murder of the king's brother, no less. How could she have been so stupid? The thought had crossed her mind at some point, but it had seemed so ridiculous she had dismissed it out of hand. Why did she not see this coming?

When she heard the soft whoosh of the door opening, she ceased her rocking and whimpering. Tears brimming in her eyes, Liv raised her face to stare at the king of the Overworld.

"Rogan is your twin brother."

Raskhan nodded.

She took a deep breath. "Why didn't you tell me?"

"Oh, kitten, I couldn't do that. I had so much fun watching you grapple with the mystery of my appearance. Boy, did I enjoy that. Not to mention the fact that it got me a fantastic view of your little ass."

She felt like grinding her teeth. She breathed, determined not to go down that road but to stay focused on crucial matters.

"But how? I don't get it. I mean, vampires can't have kin. How did this happen?"

"Does it matter? Would the explanation make you happy?"

She supposed not. Yet a part of her kicked with frustration, screamed her need to understand.

"Why do you hate him so much? You're the king, he's not. What can he possibly have done to you?"

"I've told you before. It's none of your business."

Raskhan's level tone outraged her even more than being sentenced to death. She stood up.

"I didn't kill Rogan."

"I know."

She must have looked confounded because a curious smile appeared on his face when he witnessed her expression.

"Although Khord swore you did, I'm sure he lied. Now that I've seen the way you consistently wail for my brother, I believe you'd go to great lengths to keep him alive."

"Then where is he?"

"Well, as you're here and he's not, I'd guess Khord found a way to end his miserable life."

No way would she believe that. Rogan must have been delayed, cornered, maybe trapped somewhere and unable to run to her rescue, but he was alive. He had to be. She so wanted to see him again. If she was to be executed, she needed to look on his beloved face one more time.

"Khord is the one who shot Rogan, and he almost killed him. As a rule I thought you vampires stuck together, you know, the whole vampires against humans thing. So how come that bastard Khord…?" Liv raised a hand to her mouth. "Please, don't tell me you ordered your brother's murder."

"As much as I would have liked to, that's Khord's doing. Those two never got on well. I guess it had to come to this sooner or later. What I'd like to know is how Rogan pulled it off."

"Well, I…"

Her teeth clacked as she shut her mouth. Why would she give Raskhan any information? After all she owed him nothing, and he was going to have her executed anyway.

"You what?"

Abs pulled tight to maintain her back as straight as possible, chin up, Liv didn't answer him. Her refusal must have been funny to him because the freckles glinted in his eyes as he brought a finger to her neckline and stroked the skin above her breasts.

"Come on, little girl, do I have to make you say it?"

Deadlock. She knew he was making no idle threats, but giving in twisted her guts. Or did it? Couldn't her stomach be roiling because he was now tracing her collarbone with a slow finger?

The bell didn't save Liv, but the older vampire with silver hair did. As he entered the room quietly, Raskhan backed off. Mischief playing in his magnetic eyes, he blew her a kiss.

"Don't get too worked up while I'm gone, kitten. I promise you we'll finish this later."

His mean yet sensual tone ignited a familiar sensation between her legs. Caught by desire, she bit her lip to quell her rash excitement, and watched him exit the room. Why was he leaving her with the old guy? And what was she doing here now?

Now that she had the opportunity to look around, she realised this place resembled a scientific lab. A long stainless worktable displayed microscopes and various pieces of equipment she had no name for. Holy mackerel, did they have in mind to torture her?

"My name is Zontag. Don't be scared, I won't hurt you."

He presented her with a clean, metallic bowl of some kind. She took it without thinking.

"What do you want with me?"

"I'm going to run a few tests, and I'd like you to be still. Don't worry, it won't take long."

A string of fear coiled around her throat. Liv took a step back. Her shin banged against the chair, making her wince. Seeing her evident distress, Zontag offered her a genuine smile, the first gesture of sympathy since she had been torn from her world.

"What kind of tests?"

"I need to analyse your body fluids." With a nod, he indicated a door at the back of the lab. "That's a private bathroom over there. Would you mind relieving yourself in this bowl and bring it back to me?"

By now Liv didn't need the king in the same room to know what a refusal would come to. She nodded and did what the scientist asked. Done, she watched him empty the bowl in a sort of cocktail shaker. While her pee turned blue because he had added a liquid from a small bottle, Zontag pointed to a dentist's chair. God, how she hated those reclining seats! Doing her best to push back mental images of drills and curettes, she settled on the chair.

"Why are you doing this to me?"

"I'm looking for any indication that you might be..."

He didn't finish his sentence. Switching the cocktail shaker on, he raised his head to stare at her as though he sought the solution to an insoluble problem. Whatever he saw must have incited him to reach a conclusion because he expelled a long sigh.

"I don't know what Rogan told you, but you might be the most dangerous threat vampires have ever had to face since the Dividing War. I believe you're the Bringer of Death."

There they were again, back to their prophecy crap. But for once Liv couldn't have cared less, her heart skipping a beat at the mention of Rogan's name. Body tensed, she gripped the arms of the chair and blurted out.

"Have you seen him? Do you know where he is?"

There was no mistaking her nervous tone and posture. Zontag smiled when he heard her hopeful babble, and turned off the shaker.

"Can you keep a secret?"

Liv scrambled off the dentist's chair, her black robe billowing around her legs. Elated, she rushed to the older vampire and grabbed his hand, her breath coming out in rasps. "You've seen him, haven't you?

How is he? Is he okay? Why didn't he come back to me? Where's he gone?"

"Hush now, I will tell you but I want these tests done. Take a deep breath and get back on that seat!"

Although a little reluctant, Liv did what she was told. As he studied a set of different coloured lights at the base of the shaker, Zontag began writing down numbers on a blank sheet.

"Rogan came back after his encounter with you. Or rather he sneaked back here. He didn't want anyone to know his whereabouts so we had a private meeting. He told me all about you, and how you saved his life."

"You knew, yet you didn't tell the truth to the council! Do you realise they've sentenced me to death?"

"I understand your resentment, but they won't make it final until we figure out who you are. Besides, our meeting was secret, and Rogan asked me to keep the news to myself for the time being. I'm sure he has a plan, but he didn't have time to discuss it with me."

"Did he also tell Raskhan?"

Losing sight of his calculations, Zontag gave her a sharp glance. "I'm fairly certain he wouldn't do that."

Liv wished someone would explain the nature of the relationship between the two brothers. What or who could have generated such hate? A fight for power? A female vampire? A woman? Then she swallowed when Zontag came up to her with a syringe in his hand.

"This might sting a bit, but it will be over in a sec'."

"Were Rogan and Raskhan twins back when they were still human? I'm not an expert on the matter, but I've always thought people became vampires when they were bitten by one."

Zontag brought the syringe to her arm. The needle prompted Liv to shut her eyes for a brief instant. She winced when it penetrated her flesh, although she felt almost no pain. Her eyes popping open, she saw the older vampire shake his head.

"And your assumption is correct. It so happens that Raskhan and Rogan are an oddity, the exception that proves the rule."

"What do you mean?"

His gentleness indicating he was being careful not to hurt her, he slowly drew out blood. Syringe half full in hand, he extracted it to apply a patch on the pinprick.

"They were never bitten and turned. They were born vampires."

Chapter Nineteen

"Oh, my God, is it possible?"

"If I hadn't witnessed it, I'd be as sceptical as you are."

Going around the worktable, he placed a few drops of her blood on a small slab of glass that he inserted in the closest microscope. Then he emptied the rest of the red liquid into a flask. Brow knitted, one of his hands around a knob, he studied her blood cells while he told his tale.

"The race of men won the Dividing War. They appointed the greatest enemy warrior as king and exiled all vampires into the Overworld. Assisted by a council he had selected, the king ruled over our world for thousands of years. Right until the day fate decided to claim him."

Eyes wide, all thoughts of drills and needles having left her as soon as the tale began, Liv sat up straighter in the chair.

"He fell in love with a human. She must have been about four months pregnant when they met, and the king took great pains not to harm her. However, a month later either his compulsion got the better of him or she asked him to bite her. I can't say for sure, but he did it. Such is love!"

Liv knew for sure. She had been there. She had seen Rogan battling with the overwhelming compulsion to sink his fangs into her neck. She had felt the irresistible impulse, and had commanded him to sink his fangs into her. Mindless of any consequences, she had asked to be bitten.

"The king poisoned her. Before she'd had enough time to turn into a vampire, something unexpected happened. As the vampire's venom infiltrated her blood, delivery began. I was immediately called to her side. I did my best to save her, but her weak body couldn't withstand the transformation. She died giving birth to two boys. Two tiny creatures bound to die because, by that time, the poison had already made its way into them."

"Go on, what happened?"

"A genetic abnormality. Instead of killing the boys the poison saved them. What's more, two weeks later they had reached the size and weight of regular human newborns. So the king held a council meeting to pass a law. If need be the firstborn was to succeed him."

"Why did he do that? I mean, come on, he's immortal."

"Love had slain him. When she died, she took his heart with her. The day after the council meeting, he entrusted the boys to my care. Then he went to your world and stepped out into the sunshine."

A sensation of pain pulled Liv out of Zontag's fascinating story. Vampires were capable of committing suicide out of love? She gripped the arms of the chair so hard that her skin showed the marks.

Letting out a long sigh, she rubbed her palms together.

"This is unbelievable. But about the boys, what are they?"

"I guess the best term would be 'mutants'. Their vampire abilities are stronger than any I've ever seen, but they age as humans do. I delivered them into the world thirty years ago, and so far they've evolved like men. They also feel certain things as a human would do."

"What kind of things?"

"Love, guilt, anger, sympathy, passion, jealousy. You know, the whole range of emotions. And hate."

"But vampires don't?"

"We do, just not in any way as intensely as the boys. All their senses are heightened. I'm also positive they don't need refreshing because they're mutants, but I haven't told them yet."

"Why not?"

Zontag stuck his head out to look at her, a smile illuminating his features.

"Nah, they'd get too cocky!"

Good point. Raskhan certainly was cocky enough for her taste. As interesting as their story sounded, Liv needed to ask the question that had plagued her since she had laid eyes on the king of the Overworld.

"How do you tell them apart?"

"Their voices. Rogan's tone is slightly lower-pitched than Raskhan's. Unfortunately for you, this vocal difference is too fine to be perceived by human ears. To us vampires, it's unmistakable. They speak a single word, and we know who's who."

Zontag's clarification seemed to lift a heavy weight from her shoulders. Telling them apart appeared as easy as breathing to everybody around here, and that fact had contributed to exacerbate her feeling of being out of place.

Learning her inability had everything to do with her being human somehow brought immediate relief. She was neither crazy nor irrational, she just wasn't a vampire. And considering that she still hadn't changed after two vampires' bites, she probably wouldn't be.

"Why do they hate each other?"

"It's been like this since they were children, although nobody knows for sure. If he feels so inclined, that is for one of them to tell you."

A hard plastic stick in his hand, Zontag seemed to have forgotten all about his microscope as he came to stand in front of her.

"Now, open your mouth."

With it he scraped first the inside of her cheeks before moving on to the back of her tongue. Trying not to gag, Liv let him collect whatever he needed from her saliva and mucous tissue. When he turned away to go back to his worktable, she waited until he faced her again.

"I'm not your Bringer of Death, you know."

He raised his eyebrows. "Ha ha." Then he set the stick inside a weird machine that looked somewhat like a mixer.

"I'll show you something."

As she slithered down the dentist's chair, he pressed a button on the side of his worktable. Then he gestured for her to turn around. The back wall of the lab slid open. Not the entire wall, but a square the size of a window. His hand on her back, Zontag prompted her forward.

"This is a two-way mirror. Take a look, he won't see you."

On the other side, the large room appeared to be a relaxing place of some kind, reminding Liv of a spa. Two empty brown loungers sat in front of bookcases filled with thousands of books. Apparently, some vampires spent a lot of time reading. In the far corner, two massage tables lay side by side, waiting to be used. Beside them, Liv saw a large hot tub drained of water.

"Our former king had this room equipped for the human he loved. He wanted her to spend most of her days here, and enjoy herself as if she was in her own world. Now, do you recognise him?"

In the centre of the room, a vampire sitting at a school desk was busy drawing. Although he seemed vaguely familiar, Liv didn't place him until he raised his head. But when he did, she gasped. Back in the warehouse, he had been the warrior who had come with Khord, and failed to send her to the Overworld. No way she'd ever forget his face.

"I thought you might recognise him."

"Who is he?"

"One of our hunters. Well, at least he was until yesterday."

Zontag's strange tone caused Liv to glance at him. Head a little cocked, eyes glazed from staring too hard, he appeared totally mystified by the vampire in the other room.

"What's different about him today? He looks the same to me."

"Indeed he does."

Zontag left her side to go back to his worktable and activate the closing of the two-way mirror. The panel slid shut with a barely audible sigh, blocking her view of the warrior. Turning round, palms up, she waited for the scientist to speak. He retrieved the plastic stick from the machine and placed it on the worktable.

"Rogan told me about your fight in the warehouse. He said you touched the hunter, but as nothing happened he was sent home."

"That's right. Why? Didn't he come back here?"

"He did."

"So what's the big deal?"

"He isn't a vampire anymore. He's human."

Holy mackerel, she hadn't expected that! Did Zontag mean her touch had changed a vampire into a human? Now that would be an extraordinary feat, especially considering that, at the time, the force had seemed to fail her. Or had she wrongly assumed the experience had been a failure because she didn't see any physical effect on the warrior?

"Is he the reason why everyone here seems wary of me?"

"Absolutely. He recounted the episode to the council, and, true or false, the whole community is aware of your power now. Besides Khord became an eye witness when he backed up his partner."

"Oh, the nerve of that monster! Khord had already gone when it happened. He didn't see squat!"

"Yet it's his word against yours. In such a matter, only Rogan could set the record straight."

But Rogan had disappeared. He wasn't here to stand by her side, to protect her, to save her from an impending execution. Accusing her of a crime of lese-majesty was only an excuse. Even if the council believed Rogan alive, they'd still kill her to eliminate a threat. As if reading her mind, two fingers on his chin, Zontag nodded.

"By changing vampires into humans, you have the power to eradicate our race. It means you are..."

He faltered, his blue eyes seeming a shade darker. Understanding lifting the veil she had been enfolded in, Liv finally appraised her true condition. Without a blink, she ended the sentence for him.

"I'm the Bringer of Death."

They stared at each other. About two feet apart, she closed the distance between them. Even if all clues pointed to her being some kind of vampire killer, a part of her still wanted to kick up a fuss.

"But I can't be!" The words tumbling out of her mouth, she grabbed the older vampire's hand. "You see, when Rogan was dying from Khord's silver bullet, I saved his life. I healed him."

"Rogan briefly mentioned..."

"Believe me, it's true. That's my power. I heal vampires!"

"No, you don't. I believe you healed Rogan only because he's part human. But when a true vampire is in your hands, your power destroys his essence and it all comes down to your blood being pure."

As Zontag's hand pressed her fingers tighter, she read absolute certainty in his blue eyes. He wasn't putting on a show to mislead her. He was actually telling her to acknowledge facts. As long as she'd be trapped in the Overworld, her power was the key to her survival. The scientist's hands relaxed while he carried on his explanation.

"For the same reason, a vampire's bite won't affect you because your blood can't be mixed and protects you. I told Rogan as much. Now I'd like to hear about your power. What did you feel when you healed him? And when you changed the warrior?"

As much as she wanted to describe the incredible force she had experienced when healing Rogan, her stomach interrupted her. Like a snake uncoiling from a light sleep, it roiled. Lungs deprived of air, heart fluttering to be let out, the vibe whipped her with brutal desire. Following the persistent pull of her instincts, Liv moved to face the door.

The king of all vampires barged into the room. Dark and ominous, his gaze passed over her to settle on Zontag.

"Are you done with her?"

"I am, but I'd like to work on..."

"Leave us!"

Cut short, the older vampire bowed and obeyed his king. As his hand left hers, Liv wished he wouldn't abandon her to the whims of his towering master. With a last glance at her, Zontag hurried out of the lab and closed the door behind him. Looking smug, Raskhan finally acknowledged her presence.

"I will run the last test on you."

The invisible connection instantly responded to his words. It writhed in her belly, forcing her to breathe through her mouth.

"What test?"

"Didn't Zontag say he needed your body fluids? Well, there's one you haven't given him yet, but I'll take care of that."

Raskhan took a step towards her. Wolf-like, he seemed about to pounce on her. She should have been scared. Yes, she should have been, but the vibe pulled and pulled, throwing her pulse out of sync, jolting her bones, discharging heat between her legs.

A single look at him, and she wanted the king of the Overworld to pin her down on the worktable, to spread her legs wide open for his royal cock, and to have him make a sexual slave out of her. Still, she wouldn't cave in without a fight. She wouldn't let primitive instincts best her.

"I don't understand."

His eyes shone bright. A mischievous smile playing on his full lips, he seemed to love the moment.

"Sure, you do. Come on, little girl, don't play coy with me. Take your panties off!"

Chapter Twenty

Eyes wide, Liv watched him come to her.

"Is this really necessary? I've never heard of a test involving a woman's...well, you know."

"You're in my world now, and the rules are mine to dictate. Here, you obey me. You don't think, you don't speak, you just do as I say."

She backed away from him. His magnetic gaze holding her, she retreated until the wall halted her. He advanced on her until their bodies touched. They both shivered as though an invisible, powerful current jostled them.

"Hell, you're so desirable!" For once his face showed no trace of derision — only lust.

Yet it didn't mean she'd yield to his desires. "Flattery won't get you anywhere. You can drop the pretence right now because I won't agree to your stupid test."

He laughed then. His body hard against hers, his mouth inches from her, he passed a light finger over her lips. "And you fall for it every time! I don't think I've ever met anyone as gullible as you, kitten."

Too fast for her eyes to catch, he opened the lab door before she could think of a pertinent answer. God, he had the knack of irritating her so much she'd have liked to strangle him. Or rip his heart out. Or let him possess her body like a wild animal. But he was already out on the gallery, beckoning to her.

"Come."

"Where are we going?"

"It's high time you discovered my world."

As usual, male and female servants gave them a wide berth. Along open galleries, past rows of doors, up two flights of stairs, along brightly lit corridors, Raskhan led her onto an open terrace. Situated on top of the palace, square and large, the terrace dominated the landscape — if it could be called a landscape.

Night and cold ruled. Dark, thick shadows closing in on her, Liv watched her step as she approached the ledge. An unfamiliar sensation grazed the back of her mind, and was gone before she could grasp it. Hands on the parapet, Raskhan by her side, she strained to get a good look around.

All she discerned were two-storey black buildings, squarely divided by streets. A few lights here and there showed signs of unseen presences. No houses. No towers. No skyscrapers. No flat land indicating parks or unused grounds. From where she stood, the methodically lined-up buildings reminded Liv of the ordered structures her little cousin used to build with his Lego set. No sun. No daylight. Only night.

As far as the eye could see the same arranged layout didn't leave much to the imagination. One must be very creative here to find a source of inspiration. Then again this world was so plunged in darkness she wouldn't be able to discern hidden beauties. Erected in the centre, the king's white marble palace stood out like a black hair on a fried egg.

"Are all your towns like this?"

"You're looking at the only town in the Overworld."

"How many are you?"

"We used to be a million vampires before the Dividing War. Today I'd say about twenty thousand, and all staying here."

Liv had no idea how many men had died in the same war, but obviously the ability to have children had saved the human race. The sensation she had felt earlier came back to her, making her shiver. The silence. The heavy, cold, tear-proof silence surrounding them.

"What's past the town?"

"An endless desert, and death."

She heard him. He was telling her she wouldn't survive out there. Even if she found the front door of his palace, even if she made it to the edge of town, there was no escape. No life.

This barren universe belonged to Raskhan and Rogan. More accurately, they belonged to these desolate, lonely wastelands. Did it mean they were empty, too, and devoid of lush, torrid emotions? Rogan hadn't been. The brief moment when he had spoken about the Overworld, his voice had vibrated with sorrow. Looking at Raskhan now, Liv fancied his taut features reflected the same sorrow. King or not, one thing was for sure—both brothers were cut from the same cloth. Both wanted in and out.

"Why did you bring me up here?"

"To show you what Rogan and I are like. You think you love him, but you don't know him."

Unable to tell if Raskhan's words were meant as a warning or as a hint at something she should have figured out, Liv rubbed her arms with both hands. In any case, she didn't like the way he sounded.

"I'm cold."

He shrugged. Grabbing her arm, he led her back inside the palace. This time avoiding the open galleries but using the back ways, they went straight to her bedroom. She stepped in. He stayed at the threshold and gestured towards the bed.

"There's a switch for the lights by the bed. Rest now."

"What if I'm not tired?"

Whatever sorrow or loneliness he might have felt up on the terrace vanished as she defied him. His wolf-like grin reappeared, a savage glimmer of anticipation and desire passing in his eyes. "I see. Maybe you'd like me to entertain you for a while. Is that what you're asking me, little girl?"

She could have slapped herself for being so stupid. She ought to have known by now that Raskhan was nothing but a predator, and that any excuse to pounce on his prey would do. Damn her big mouth. "No, thanks, I'll be fine."

Taking a long inspiration to settle the bumpy cadence of her heart, Liv turned her back on the king of the Overworld. Only when she heard the door shutting did she let some air out of her lungs.

A quick shower and she felt much better. She dried off her hair with a towel before jumping into bed. Fresh linen welcoming her naked body, she stretched her weary limbs and yawned. She then curled up on her side, knees drawn up.

She had lied to Raskhan. As she found the switch to turn the lights off, tiredness had already filled her bones. Bathed in complete darkness, pictures of Rogan invaded her mind when she closed her eyes.

His unconscious body lying on her couch while she healed him from the silver bullet. His face when he had fought Khord to save her life. The wonderful feel of his mouth on hers, the way he kissed her like no man ever had. His scream of utter pleasure as he came inside her, night and woods shielding them from the rest of the world.

But images of Raskhan muddled up her memories as she drifted off to sleep. Her face against the bathroom door, the king's finger fondling her sex, igniting a wild desire she hadn't yet come to terms with. His roguish expression when she had realised he wasn't the same vampire her heart was beating for. And always there, the irresistible connection between them.

Liv dreamt. High above their heads, the sun nurtured plants, trees, fields, and forests. Sitting by a brook Rogan motioned her to come to him, his thoughtful gaze and loving smile fixed on her. Although she walked, she didn't seem to get any closer to the vampire she loved. In spite of her desperate need to feel his arms around her, to be kissed by his overriding mouth, the distance between them grew farther. As a last resort, she began running to him.

She ran, but he receded from her. As much as she wanted to call his name, no sound came out of her lips. Around her the beautiful clearing seemed to take on a new dimension. A hush fell over the forest as if nature was taking a break. The brook only a dot on the horizon, her heart beating too fast, she slowed her pace to a vacillating walk.

Stepping out of the dense forest, Raskhan pointed a finger at her. Mesmerised by his commanding gesture, she moved towards him. Every step she took aroused a deep longing in her loins, an unfathomable yearning in her soul. Then the vibe took possession of her senses, and her body erupted in desire.

Torn out of her dream by this violent sensation, Liv felt his stony chest pressed on her back, his legs moulded against hers, one of his hands cupping her breast, his erect shaft wedged between her thighs. Sleep abandoned her in a rush of moistness. His blatant lust ensnared her, and a single thought overruled her mind. She wanted him.

"I know you're awake."

How could he not? Although total darkness enfolded them, his thumb brushing her nipple, mere inches from the pounding of her heart, from the erratic rise and fall of her chest. How could he not know she was wide awake as his tongue seared a line from her right shoulder to her left?

"I want you so badly."

A tremor of anticipation coursed through her. Beyond the obvious sexual intent Raskhan's admission pleased her in a way she hadn't expected. Like he was yielding some ground. Like he was expressing a real emotion. But why should she care about his feelings?

"Open up for me, kitten."

As unbelievable as it sounded, he was asking her permission. She still lay on her side but, in her sleep, she had stretched her legs. His simple request inflamed her from head to toe, and she reacted instinctively. She drew her knees up, baring her opening to his intense desire.

He twirled her rigid nipple with two fingers as she moved her legs up to let him in. Slow but confident, his erection glided past her buttocks to find its way to her throbbing sex.

"Yes, that's it. Hell, you're so wet for me!"

His dirty talk set her on fire. Because she hadn't seen it the first time he had screwed her, she imagined his long dick about to penetrate her, coarse hair circling the base, soft skin crowning the tip. Would he be as rough as he had been in the motel bedroom? Had he planned to fuck her, only to humiliate her later? She needn't have wondered because when he slid his steely sex into her, she thought she might choke from pleasure.

"Can you feel my cock, kitten? Tell me, do you like my big hard cock inside you?"

Her whole body screamed yes, and she had to squeeze her lips tight to keep from replying. Still cuddling her nipple, he pushed his burning rod all the way in, flattening her bum against his pelvis.

"I know you do, you little vixen. You desire me so much I can't think of anything else but your tight pussy around my dick."

Although he moved slowly up and down, his sex seemed to grow bigger with each penetration, his crude language propelling her at lightning speed to a paroxysm of pleasure. The prolonged intensity of his passion captured her mind, transformed her into a burning torch. As he strengthened his motions in and out of her, then bent her slightly forward to get a better angle and a firmer grip on her, she moaned.

"You like that, don't you? You like what I'm doing to you. Do you want more of my juicy cock, kitten? It's for you, it's all for you."

As if he knew she wouldn't reply, he nibbled her shoulder. She didn't feel his fangs but the gentle grazing of his teeth caused a new rush of moistness. Darkness hid his next move, but also allowed her to feel instead of seeing. He removed his hand from her breast to bring it to his mouth. She heard sucking sounds as he licked his fingers before reaching for her breasts again.

He pinched her nipple once more, but his saliva smoothed his touch as his fingers stroked until her nerves twitched. Pinned to the mattress by the exquisite rubbing and the whole length of his cock buried inside her, she felt on the verge of losing her mind. Mouth agape to draw in much needed air, she couldn't suppress a groan. As if hearing her cry stimulated him, his dick stiffened and he pressed his pelvis against her back.

"Fuck! You're so hot I could spend my time making love to you. And, damn it, your pussy is so tight and smooth. It makes me want to bang you every fucking minute."

Although his dirty talk excited her beyond imagining, his use of a special expression brought a new moan to her lips. In the midst of passion, in a rare moment when truth came forth, he had said he was making love to her. And the strangest thing was that she believed him.

Her heart was about to burst from joy. She couldn't tell if it was from sexual enjoyment or from happiness at hearing such words, so she arched her body against his.

"Oh yes, that's it. Come to me."

Her luscious movement stirred a new rigidity in her cunt. How much harder could he get? In response he freed her nipple to slide his hands around her waist. Using her hips to slightly lift her up, he pushed his dick in and out of her to the point where tears stung her eyes. Then she began panting like a bitch in heat as the stirrings of an orgasm raised all the hair on her body.

"Listen hard now, kitten. You're mine, do you hear me? You're nobody else's but mine!"

And he wouldn't relent. Using his thumbs, he applied pressure on her back to make her lean forward. She uttered a high-pitched keen when he drove his sex right up, picking up speed as he possessed her body and mind.

"I'm gonna burst out in you. I want to hear you come, and I'm gonna splatter your hot pussy with my spunk."

This time she felt his mouth brush her neck, his fangs pierce her skin, his cock palpitate with impending release. But his lewd words toppled her over the abyss. When his final thrusts bombed her flesh, spasms of stupendous pleasure heaved her body, and she cried out Rogan's name.

His limbs quivered as he discharged into her, a single satisfied grunt passing through his lips. Then his tongue lapped her neck before he enveloped her with his strong arms. She stayed there without moving, feeling his sex slowly retreating out of her, enjoying the safe sensation of his embrace.

So exhausted she didn't think she'd able to lift a finger, she closed her eyes. Now wasn't the time to dwell on the name she had shouted, or on the impact it might have had on Raskhan. First she needed to forget they had made love. But as sleep drew her towards oblivion, she heard his last whisper.

"Why don't you love me?"

Chapter Twenty-One

Liv was alone in bed when she woke up. She hit the switch, and light flooded the room. What time could it be? Although she felt rested, it might still be the middle of the night for all she knew. Except that in this world daylight would never come. If she ever got back home, her first move would be to buy a watch. No concession. Buy a watch and keep track of time.

She got up to check her handbag, and locate her cellphone. No signal, of course. What were the odds? But the screen displayed the time and she hadn't expected anything else. Ten past six p.m. Did that count as oversleeping on a Monday afternoon? Or was it already Tuesday? Left to her own devices in this dark world, she'd end up drawing signs up the wall to estimate the passing of days. Having no other use for it, she turned her phone off.

In the bathroom, she inspected her neck. She had been bitten three times, yet barely a vague scar showed. Even if a magic healing spell had been cast on her, it wouldn't have worked faster. But as smooth as her skin looked and felt, a pang of regret hit her.

Rogan's bite mark was gone without a trace, erased from her flesh. Now only her recollections of him remained clear.

Averting her eyes, Liv cleaned up and donned the black robe she had been given. She didn't think her regular clothes would fit in well in the palace. When not going on a mission into her world, everybody here wore black robes except Raskhan. Not chic enough for a powerful, uncompromising king? A king who had rendered her delirious with passion last night.

Holy mackerel, how she had fallen asleep again after their torrid lovemaking she had no idea. On the other hand, she was totally aware of the name she had shouted when Raskhan had brought her to climax. Any chance he hadn't heard it? Yeah, she wished!

First of all, leniency and forgiveness didn't appear to be the king's forte. On second thought she had now presented him with a valid, legitimate reason to have her executed. Thrown into a new, unbelievable universe, one might have used one's time to study its laws, rules and workings. But not her. Oh, no, she was too busy digging her own grave!

A rumbling rose from her stomach. Toast and scrambled eggs came to mind, shooting her morning hunger to a higher level. Although three times bitten, Liv reckoned Zontag was right about her blood protecting her from becoming a vampire. Nonetheless she was hungry.

As she came out of the bathroom, someone knocked on the door. Raskhan? She briefly considered hiding, but where? Overlooking the fact that she wasn't five years old anymore to play hide and seek, she didn't feel the vibe. No vibe, no Raskhan. As simple as that. Besides, the king had never knocked on her door before. The king simply barged in, or crept into her bed uninvited.

Trusting her instincts, she opened the door to a female vampire carrying a tray of food. The silent servant handed her the tray, then scurried down the hallway. Okay. From time to time, this Bringer of Death stuff had its uses.

No scrambled eggs, but bread, butter and pastries did the trick. Belly full, she washed her late afternoon breakfast down with hot coffee from a large takeaway paper cup. Holding it, she wondered who had gone over to her beautiful, sunny world to get some food. She wished Raskhan had sent Khord to run this errand on her account. After shooting Rogan and insulting her, that ugly bastard well deserved this kind of punishment.

Pushing images of Khord away, Liv emptied the contents of her bag on the bed. First she did her nails then got absorbed in the crossword book she always kept with her. For a long while, the brain puzzles kept her away from her confused state of mind.

When she got bored with crosswords, she sat at the writing desk. Who knew, she might not have another opportunity to look at the ancient book of prophecy. She pulled out the precious manuscript from the drawer, her fingers light on the worn-out leather bindings. Wasn't it very convenient to find this book just lying there in an unlocked drawer? Right in the room where she had been assigned. Oh well, better use it than lose a good opportunity to learn about the immortal race.

She hadn't bookmarked the passage so she began thumbing through the pages. After a while she became aware that she wasn't paying any attention to the task at hand. Her mind kept wandering to other things, preventing her from finding mentions of the Bringer of Death. Not quite right, given that her musing basically focused on Raskhan's last question.

Why don't you love me?

Although he had whispered it at the time, the question still rang loud and clear in her head. Where did this issue come from? What had initiated it? And what did it mean? As she pondered the problem, the letters blurred and the book of prophecy seemed to increase in size.

Why didn't she love him? Because she loved Rogan. Because Raskhan was a self-satisfied, cynical, wicked, mischievous, irritating ruler who was using her to achieve his secret purpose and who had sentenced her to death. Because in a wink he had figured out her weaknesses and loved to play with them. Because he was an arrogant, selfish...

Liv took a long breath. She could carry on like this for hours and the list might never end. To sift out the truth from the lies, she needed to concentrate. Did she really? How about giving her emotions free rein and letting her intuition guide her? No, no good. If she shut off her pragmatic approach to the mystery that was Raskhan, if she allowed herself to not think and just feel, then she'd be forced to bring into reality something she didn't want to see.

Yes, the king of the Overworld was all of those things but somewhere along the line she had discovered he was a real person. Zontag's narration of the brothers' birth had unleashed emotions she had only felt so far for Rogan. And last night had changed everything. She had trembled with passion in Raskhan's arms, and for one precious moment she had believed he cared.

Dear God, please, let it not be true. She couldn't harbour feelings for Raskhan. No good could come out of that, and it would be a real disaster. Come on, she hated his guts! And why wasn't Rogan here when she needed him? Why had he left her at the hands of his so damn exciting vampire brother?

Well, Rogan wouldn't give her the answer. She'd have to deal with her ambiguous emotions on her own. How was she supposed to do that with the goddamn vibe writhing in her belly every time Raskhan got close to her? Did he want her to feel for him? Was he in love with her? Holy mackerel, she needed a vacation.

Shaking her head, Liv bent over the book of prophecy. Different drawings and sentences looked the same to her, similar pages somehow appeared disparate. Even in a good cheerful mood, she wouldn't have been able to figure out anything from that old jumble. She had to stop wasting her time. Yet, as pointless as it seemed, she felt pulled to the ancient book.

She was about to turn yet another page when a particular entry caught her eye. Capital letters had been used to write the first letters of both words, and the spelling had her mind racing—*the Rogue and the Rascal*. The rest of the sentence was written in a cryptic language but ten lines down she found a new mention—*the Rascal and the Rogue*.

Wow! No need to be an expert in ancient languages to decipher that one. As if under an enchanting spell, she spoke the words aloud. "The rascal and the rogue. Raskhan and Rogan."

Liv checked the next page in hopes of stumbling across a more meaningful section. No such luck as only page after page of illegible doodle met her eye.

She closed the book. Putting it back in the drawer, she wondered about fate. Were Raskhan and Rogan meant to accomplish something? Maybe some kind of quest to save their world? Against all odds, why were they mentioned in the same manuscript as the Bringer of Death? Did it mean they were destined to dispose of their enemy? So far, they had both done the exact opposite. Unless making love to their enemy counted as a disposal.

Brushing her hair back, Liv sighed. The whole business started to get too tricky for her taste. So many things she didn't understand and how many more to come? She stood up, and pushed the chair back to stretch her legs. When she turned round her blood iced in her veins.

His horrid face displaying a satisfied sneer, his hand around a long vicious-looking knife, Khord stood by the bedroom door.

Chapter Twenty-Two

Engrossed in her discovery, she hadn't heard the soft sound of the door opening—too late now. Sweat sticking her armpits, Liv swallowed while evaluating her chances of escape. As he was positioned between her and the door, she figured there were none. Then the monster approached his prey, a heinous grin twisting his features.

He was a vampire warrior. She was a human being, and a woman at that. If she hoped to get out of this situation in one piece she had to be stronger than him. She had to act as if she was in command. Pointing a finger at him, she did the only thing she could think of.

"Get out!"

He snorted. She read hate in the malevolence of his nasty stare. She read murder in the readiness of his stance. A cold sensation creeping in her bones, she kept still but didn't dare take her eyes off him.

"Not so brash now, are you? Why is that, I wonder? You were way more confident when Rogan was around."

She didn't reply. She didn't bat an eyelash. He was taunting her to scare the hell out of her, but she wouldn't fall into his obvious trap. Or maybe he was just being his regular idiotic self. Whatever, his sneer deepened as if a thought had just crossed the blobby thing he called his brain.

"By the way, where is lover boy? Apparently not here to save you this time. Well, I'm not surprised. I mean who would stick around a whore like you, fucking his brother and all?"

She felt punched below the belt. She breathed through her mouth to remain motionless, and to pretend she didn't give a damn about his accusations. But she did, and the blow landed hard.

"I bet he won't take it well. He's a dork all right but, come on, his girlfriend is humping his own brother. Got to cut the man some slack."

"Shut up, you stupid pig!"

As much as she wanted to keep a cool composure, Khord's cheap shot hit her like a slap in the face.

"If you kill me the king will know you did it."

Khord guffawed. Then he screwed up his eyes as if he had been expecting this kind of retort. "How? You won't be there to tell him. Besides, he believes I'm like all the others, scared shitless of you because you're some sort of vampire killer. You don't look much like a killer to me."

"Well, I am!"

"Sure you are. Just like you're faithful to lover boy!"

Liv had been wrong in assuming every vampire in the palace feared her. The brute opposite her didn't. She could see it in his evil glare, and in the way his fingers gripped the blade. But, as she looked from the sharp knife back to his bloodthirsty face, Khord caught her glance.

"I see you've met my friend. Good, 'cause this won't take a minute!"

Instead of backing away, Liv tried to slip past him to get a better shot at the door.

He watched her, his features shifting to his vampire face, his ugliness even more enhanced.

But once the bedroom door lay to her left side, she realised the uselessness of her spur-of-the-moment plan. Even if she had been standing downstairs in the grand hall, he'd still be faster than her. Then her insides locked as Khord raised the knife. He had the means to tear her throat out, but he would cut into her flesh to avoid biting marks.

For a second it felt like another Liv was watching the scene from above. Two enemies facing each other, on the brink of attacking, gazes glued. Then the second passed, and her body ached from tension. Stomach constricted with fear, she prepared to die.

"Get out!"

At the sound of Raskhan's harsh order, Khord whirled round. Instantly adopting a soldier's obedient attitude, he bowed and lowered the hand holding the knife. Then he dropped to one knee.

"At your command, my king."

Although he had just been about to slice her throat, he acted like nothing was out of place, like maybe he had popped by to give her good news. How could the king fall for such an act?

But Raskhan was looking at her and ignoring Khord. His back straight, the murderous warrior stood up and walked to the door. Just before taking off he shot Liv a final deadly glance. Still rigid with fear, she nonetheless matched his stare until he disappeared. Whichever world she breathed in, she knew that Khord wasn't yet done with her.

Liv's legs gave way under her. She'd have crumpled to the floor if Raskhan hadn't already been by her side to steady her in his arms. Her lungs hurt when she let in gulps of air. Her guts contracted with violent relief. Dear God, she was still alive. Her cheek pressed against the king's chest, she listened to the low beat of his heart.

He had a heart. Of course he had, he was half mortal. Mixed blood ran in his veins, warming his skin, giving him a human core. Regular as clockwork, the slow but potent cadence assuaged her fears. Soon she felt comforted enough to raise her face to him. Bad move as the nearness of his full lips struck a different chord in her. Forcing herself to look him in the eye, she wavered when he clutched her a little tighter.

"He won't bother you anymore."

Bother? Had he really said 'bother' or was she hearing voices? Like what had just transpired in the room had only been a minor inconvenience? The brute had been about to murder her, for crying out loud!

"He tried to kill me."

"Nah, he was just goofing around. He isn't particularly fond of you, but he wouldn't take any rash action."

Oh, swell! Now instead of taking her side, the king stood by his soldier. Sure, what else? After all, who was she to throw wild accusations to his face against one of his race? Nobody but a woman sentenced to death by a bunch of prejudiced vampires.

Anger and frustration welling up, her body tensed. Like a reflex, he slid his hands down her back, closing in on her buttocks. She pushed his arms away and took a step back.

His golden eyes glinted as he let her go. "Well, well, little girl, you weren't so touchy last night."

She felt like clamping her hand on his mouth to shove his words back down his throat. At the same time she experienced an intense need to go hang herself. She had nurtured the notion that they had shared something, that last night had been special to him too. God, she was so off the mark! "Leave me alone. I don't wanna talk about it."

A grin broke out on his face. Although he didn't make a move, she got the impression he had closed the short distance between them. Looking smug, he tilted his head.

"What if I do?"

"I'm not interested in your opinion."

"And I think you are."

Mere inches from his body, the vibe fluttered, reminder of very real sensations. Whether she acknowledged her feelings for him or not, her desire for this man would always be there, buried in her. But if he had a human heart, why didn't he use it to be gentle to her?

"Believe me, I'm not."

"Don't lie to me, kitten. You're dying to hear me say I loved doing you. For your information, I did."

"Do you have to be so blunt?"

The sly grin deepened. Although she never got what she wanted, she certainly appeared very good at entertaining him. Eyebrows raised, he used her very words against her.

"Blunt? Is that what you call it in this pretty little head of yours? I'd gathered you liked it rough, but I didn't know you also liked it dirty."

A tongue of fire shot up her cheeks, but she ignored it. Balling her hands into fists, Liv summoned her most condescending expression to look down her nose at the king of the Overworld.

"And I didn't know you wanted to be loved."

Chapter Twenty-Three

An awkward silence stretched for what seemed like hours before he strode to the door.

"Come!"

His sharp command intrigued her way more than a long speech would have done. What was on his mind now? Hurrying to catch up with him, she followed the vampire king down to the grand entrance hall. Oblivious of the quiet bustle around them, he took a watch out of one of his pockets.

"What's your address?"

He began punching in numbers even before she had finished reciting her address. He repeated the process on his own watch, then fastened the travelling device around her wrist. Was he really taking her home? Back to her glorious, lively, friendly universe?

She winced when he twisted her wrist a little too hard. Unable to decide whether he thought she might run away or attempt to stay in the Overworld, she endured his strong grip. Without a last look around, she closed her eyes just in time. Like it had occurred on her first trip, she heard the same weird whooshing sound as a slight nauseating sensation passed through her.

Although night ruled over here, too, Liv smiled with happiness. She could hear the faraway monotonous noise of traffic on the highway, the insistent chatter of a neighbouring television set, the high-pitched wails of cats mating. Even the smell of garbage elicited a happy smile. She was home.

The transportation device must've been very precise because, when she opened her eyes, they were in front of her small house. She climbed the steps, Raskhan's fingers still gripping her wrist.

"Would you let go, please? I won't run away."

He complied, but beckoned her to get inside. As always he'd only be satisfied when he got what he wanted. Making a great show of massaging her unmarred skin, she puckered her lips.

"It's locked. I don't have the keys."

He grabbed the knob, and turned it without even trying. A brutal clack informed Liv her locks would never serve again in this life, but the front door swung open. In the living room, her heart sank when she turned the lights on and realised the extent of the damage.

Everything had happened so fast that she hadn't given any thought to her home after Rogan and Khord's big fight. Furniture displaced, overturned or broken, the place still resembled a battlefield. But she wouldn't have been so bummed if Raskhan hadn't raised an eyebrow.

"Someone had his fun."

"You think this is funny?"

"Let's see, it goes with your broken door now."

Turning her back on him, she walked to the other side of the living room while assessing the damage.

She only stopped when she reached the open kitchen door.

"Why don't you tell me what we're doing here?"

"You're going to make sure nobody from your world will come looking for you."

A small lump scratched the back of her throat, making her swallow. Slowly rotating on her feet, she faced him.

"Why?"

"Because I'm going to kill you."

She crashed against the doorjamb. Legs buckling under her, she clumsily clutched the jamb to keep her balance. Breaths coming out in rasps, heart knocking on hell's door, eyes widening, she managed to mumble a few words. "You're going to kill me?"

Arms crossed over his chest, he burst out laughing. "No, but you should see the look on your face. Man, it's so worth it!"

Catching sight of a broken lamp lying on a shelf not two feet away from her, Liv leapt towards it. She grabbed the base, threw her arm back and hurled the lamp at him.

Her missile hit the target dead on. That was, if the target hadn't been inhumanly fast. Instead, the lamp struck the wall with a loud shattering noise. And Raskhan already stood in front of her, unharmed.

Still in the throes of her explosive anger, she raised her fists and pummelled his chest. At once, she grasped the full meaning of the expression 'bang one's head against a brick wall'. Within seconds, her fingers began to hurt. Then she quit hitting him as he placed his hands on her shoulders.

"Hey, calm down. I was just kidding."

She pushed his hands away, tears welling up. But, for the love of God, she wouldn't cry in front of him.

"Oh, yeah, because that was so funny!"

Unfazed by her rejection, he cocked his head like a cute puppy asking to be loved again.

"Cheer up, it wasn't that bad. Can't you tell a joke from a fact? You know I wouldn't kill you."

"No, I don't know that. You and your buddies have already sentenced me to death, and they don't look like a kidding bunch to me. You're the king, so what stops you from bringing forward my execution?"

"You're right, that's a thought."

Had he looked serious she might have believed him again. But the puppy face was still on, and his eyes glinted. Her former rage receding to the back of her mind, she sighed.

"Why are you harassing me? What have I ever done to you to deserve such a treatment?"

"Spare the rod and spoil the child."

"What? I hope you don't expect me to believe that? God, you're so full of crap sometimes!"

"Only sometimes? I'm flattered you think so highly of me."

"Oh, cut it out, would you?"

Even when he sounded good-humoured he still managed to provoke her — especially when he laughed again. "What you said is true though. I am the king of the Overworld. I can have you executed any time I want, but I can also hold it off as long as I wish. I guess it all depends on you."

"Meaning?"

"Well, you know… If you behave like a good girl, if you're nice to me, I might forget about your crime."

Unbelievable. He had just threatened to kill her to scare the hell out of her, and now he wanted to get laid? No way that was about to happen. He wouldn't mould her like clay between his fingers.

"In my world, your so-sweet proposition is called blackmail. Look, you're well aware I didn't commit any crime so why would I be" — she quoted with her fingers — "nice to you?"

"Didn't you hear what I said? I am the king."

Yeah, he was as arrogant and domineering as a vampire supreme monarch was supposed to be. For everything he did to her she should loathe him. But every time his intense gaze turned to her she felt weak at the knees. Despite his infuriating manners and in spite of not being her Rogan, he had somehow found his way into her heart.

There. The sentiment that she had strived so hard to cast out had finally come to the surface. At his mercy in a ransacked house she could only feel the tumultuous beating of her heart, and an imperious need for his affection. Holy mackerel, wasn't she in a fine mess?

"I heard you, and I choose death."

Her bragging elicited a reaction she hadn't expected. Although he didn't reach out, a flash of light crossed his eyes and his sudden stiffness told Liv he wanted her. Right there, right then. Walking away to switch the lights on in the kitchen, she went in search of a hot drink.

She made some coffee, doing her best to avoid glancing towards the living room. What was he doing in there? As she poured coffee into a mug, she brutally recalled doing the exact same thing in Rogan's company before Khord erupted into her house. Could it be a sign? A sign of what?

Liv had ample time to finish drinking her coffee before Raskhan walked into the kitchen, his features devoid of any trace of desire. He must have sweated it out. As if nothing out of the ordinary had taken place, he used his most regal air to snap his fingers towards the phone.

In all likelihood they really had come here to cover her tracks. Leaning over she grabbed the receiver, dialled her work number, and left a message on the answering machine. Her colleagues would get it first thing in the morning so nobody would come snooping around.

Back in Chicago, her parents wouldn't expect a call from her for another week. What about her sister? Even if she phoned, chances were Dawn wouldn't get worried if she didn't call back. Not for the next forty-eight hours. As for emergencies, what would be would be.

Her car was still parked in the clean motel's parking lot, but with the room paid for and so many other vehicles around nobody should give it a second look, at least for a few days. They'd simply assume she had gone without leaving a tip. And what if they called the cops? What bad would it do her?

When she hung up, Raskhan looked satisfied. As if she was alone in the room, she washed her mug, wiped the table, and busied herself with the garbage bin. He watched her do her chores without comment, his impassive features causing her to wonder what his next move would be — until he casually leaned against the sink, and inquired in an amused voice.

"I hope you don't plan to clear up the whole house."

"Would you let me?"

"As a matter of fact, I was thinking your bed may need some taking care of. What do you say, kitten?"

"I say I'll take the trash out."

Giving him a bland look, she apologised a second later as she deliberately bumped the bin liner into his legs.

"Oh, I'm sorry, your Majesty!"

Heedless of what he might say or do next, she walked to the front door and went down the few steps. She dropped the bag and ran.

Chapter Twenty-Four

What the heck had gone through her mind? What could have urged her to take such a rash, nonsensical action? Even if her unpredictable flight had taken him by surprise, he was way faster than her and well-versed in the art of tracking prey. Nonetheless, she ran.

She had thirty seconds at most to get a head start before she'd have to look for a place to hide. If Raskhan was anything like his brother and fellow vampires, he wouldn't be able to smell her. With any luck, these thirty seconds could well turn out to be her best chance of getting away from him, the real question being did she honestly want to escape him?

Legs pumping, black robe flying behind her, Liv rounded the corner of her street. Too superstitious to glance back, she focused on the way ahead, on the next intersection that would lead her away from him. In this residential neighbourhood the crisscrossing of streets formed a huge maze, and might well turn to her advantage.

When she barrelled along another street, she still didn't waste a second to look back. What she didn't see couldn't be considered real. Giving silent thanks to the dark night concealing her, she concentrated on her breathing. Her lungs hurt and the muscles in her legs didn't seem happy to endure such a rough treatment.

But Liv kept on running. Dashing past lit houses, she turned left onto another street. In spite of a hot rush of adrenaline coursing through her veins, she realised she wouldn't be able to keep up this mad gallop forever. Her speed had already decreased. Thank God she wasn't living in a mountain town with slopes instead of flat ground.

At the end of the street there were no more lights ahead, but she discerned tall trees in an endless patch of darkness. The park!

Mouth wide open to gulp in burning air, sweat wetting her armpits and fully aware of her leg's constant protest, Liv shot towards the vast expanse of grassland. If she could make it to the park, crawling under thick bushes would be a child's play. There she'd be able to get her breath back and give her aching muscles some semblance of deliverance. And then what? Was she going to spend the rest of her life cowering under bushes?

Redoubling her efforts, Liv bolted towards the park. Her whole body about to quit on her, she gritted her teeth to ignore the acute pain in her side. Although it felt like someone had run a dagger through her, she didn't slow down until she reached the gate. Forced to stop to open it, she did glance back this time. Nothing but deep silence all around and deserted streets. No sign of pursuit. At once a glimmer of hope touched her heart.

Mindful of any clue she might leave, she closed the gate behind her and sprinted towards the tall trees. Shards of pain coursing throughout her body, she remembered why she hated running in the first place.

Past the first rows of cedar trees, a dense growth of bushes appeared suitable for what she had in mind. She covered the remaining distance at a trot, sweat coating her face, her hand pressed to her side. Hearing her puffing and huffing, she understood how the three little pigs must have felt when chased down by the big bad wolf.

Heart pounding from exertion, Liv finally reached the coveted bushes. All she had to do now was wriggle underneath, but first she checked her surroundings one last time — definitely no sign of pursuit. If she had indeed given Raskhan the slip, she was good! Oh, so good!

She knelt on the grass behind the bushes while trying to get her breath back, then got down on all fours to locate the best hiding spot. To her right she spied some kind of gap in the vegetation. And she crawled towards it. And he whispered in her ear.

"Peekaboo!"

She shrieked. Her heart leapt up to the back of her throat then dropped down again. Her limbs quivered from the shock of hearing his voice so close, but her mind instantly registered two shoes by her side. Despite her insane run and the discomfort she had suffered, what hurt most at that instant was the sound of his genuine laughter.

"Wow! That was so much fun! Can we do it again?"

"Oh, shut up, you... You...!"

Liv just stayed put as pain flared up when she attempted to move.

"Okay, but if you don't want to play anymore you'd better get up. I mean, we wouldn't want me to take your position as an open invitation."

Realising she was still on all fours, she figured out in a wink what was going on in that excited mind of his. The ache in her side dulled with each passing second. She straightened up to sit on her heels. But when he took her elbow to pull her up she uttered an "Ouch" of pain.

If he hadn't held her against him she wasn't sure she'd have stayed on her feet. In the crook of his arms, she looked straight over his shoulder to avoid his intense gaze. When he spoke, his diverted tone didn't lessen the weight of his words.

"Were you trying to run away from me, little girl?"

"I wouldn't dream of it. Actually I was going down to the store to get a carton of milk."

Something stiffened against her belly, confirming her suspicions that he got excited every time she defied him. Right now the nearness of his mouth excited her too. He was going to kiss her and what would she do? But as her pulse quickened at the simple idea of being kissed by the king of the Overworld, he swept her off the ground.

"Give me your hand, my little vixen."

She complied, and he pressed buttons on both their watches. For once, she didn't close her eyes. One second they were standing in the quiet park, the next they were back in the hallway of his palace. Although they must have appeared out of nowhere servants bowed their heads to him, and carried on their usual activity. None of them looked surprised to see Liv in his arms.

Barking orders to one of them, Raskhan carried her to the room she had discovered when talking to

Zontag. The vampire turned human must have found different living quarters for the place was empty. None too gently Raskhan put her down on the nearest lounger, and removed her watch before striding back to the door.

"Wait here."

He hadn't been gone for two minutes when a servant came in to prepare the hot tub. Watching the busy vampire, Liv suddenly longed for a bath. The spa was ready when Raskhan came back. Snapping his fingers to get the servant out, he turned to her and indicated the tub.

"Enjoy it as long as you want. Nobody will disturb you."

If he hadn't been so hard on her in the past few days, she might have thought his proposition pretty touching and sweet. But the king never did anything out of the goodness of his heart. With a knowing, slanted grin, she raised her index finger to point at the two-way mirror corresponding to the lab where Zontag had run some tests on her.

"I like my privacy. Would you mind closing it?"

His face showed no trace of disappointment or surprise at her knowledge of the mirror. Nodding, he used a lever by the door to activate a sliding panel that covered the two-way mirror. Then he tilted his head towards a closet in the corner of the room.

"You'll find bath towels in there."

With that, he was gone before she could thank him. Yet she didn't waste a moment to discard her black robe, bra and panties. She stepped into the hot tub, and slid down with a sigh of satisfaction. Not too hot, not too cold, the water felt just wonderful.

The tub was big enough for her to sit back and stretch her legs. About a foot behind her two grab-handles built into the spa made her grin. They looked like the top part of swimming pool ladders, but she figured they allowed easy access. On each side, soap, shampoo, conditioner, and bath salts of all kinds and colours were displayed on a small wooden platform. To top it all the water also kept a constant perfect temperature.

Although she had the presence of mind to face the door, Liv didn't believe a vampire would dare disturb her. The king had given orders and everybody obeyed him. She soaked for a while, then fiddled around to use jet massages with different speeds. And it had taken a trip to the Overworld to get acquainted with the fantastic power of a hot tub! With a dreamy smile she let the bubbling massage pattern work its magic on her body.

She had no idea how long she had been floating in the relaxing water when the door opened. As Raskhan entered the room, Liv realised she had been feeling the vibe but had got it mixed up with the wonderful, exciting sensations stroking her body. Like an obvious fact, she understood why she hadn't felt it in the park and when Khord had tried to kill her. Violent emotions like terror or pain seemed to tone it way down.

His face unreadable, the king of the Overworld touched a switch. The light from the walls dimmed to nothing, plunging the room in total darkness. Another switch and small lights came on directly from the bottom and the sides of the hot tub. Deep shadows reigning over them, a languid hush seemed to unite with the soft radiance enlivening the spa.

Water lapping her naked body, Liv rested the back of her head on the rim and closed her eyes. Dear God, but this felt so good! Dear God, but she so wanted him to join her!

Chapter Twenty-Five

The loud thump of shoes being kicked off drew her deeper into a decidedly arousing state. She saw first his bare chest, then she watched the swift motion of his hands working on the button of his jeans. She glared at him, recalling his passionate taste for defiance. But her feigned scowl went wide of the mark as he was too busy getting out of his pants.

"What do you think you're doing?"

"Rescuing you from drowning."

Never a dull moment with him! As he pulled down his underpants, she averted her gaze. Had he been in her shoes he would have drunk in her nudity. Staring at the bubbling water, she willed herself not to look up. Seconds later he slid into the tub while she moved her legs to make room for him. His muscular body disappeared under the frothy water. Sighing, he stretched his arms out onto the rim, and gave her a large smile.

"Doesn't this feel good?"

"Fantastic, but you could have waited until I'm done."

"What? And miss an opportunity to put you in an awkward position and to enjoy the sight of your rosy cheeks? Don't you know me at all?"

Liv realised she was getting to know him well when she wondered which cheeks he was referring to. The vibe roiling in her belly, she looked at his face. A pang of disappointment hit her as she saw no trace of desire there. Knees drawn up, he kept his legs to himself and didn't try to touch her. Had he really come in here just to have a bath?

"I know what you want, kitten, but I'm worn out. All this chasing and running has taken a lot out of me."

Her cheeks heated up at least ten degrees and genuine embarrassment ran through her. Vampires didn't get tired, especially not him. He was teasing her again, yet she was powerless to control her body's natural reactions.

"First of all, I don't want anything from you. Furthermore, how did you find me in the park?"

"Given that I never lost you, I didn't 'find' you. How could I? You were as loud as a freight train. Having said that, rest assured I'll play hide-and-seek with you anytime."

And he grinned as she silently cursed him. Damn his vampire's heightened senses! Damn his excessive complacency! He didn't want her, did he? Well, it was high time she gave him a taste of his own medicine. Sitting up straighter, Liv took a long breath to enhance her breasts. His grin dwindled as her nipples broke the surface of the bubbling water.

"You know what, your Majesty? I think I'll get back to my room now. Enjoy your bath!"

She stood up with a slow, graceful move. The small lights coming from the tub glowed on her bare skin.

Her body dripping with water, she leisurely raised her arms up to wring out her hair. At her feet, the king stared hard. Jaws tensed, gaze riveted to her gleaming body, he stared at the sight of her hands wiping droplets off her breasts.

"Stop calling me 'your Majesty' and sit down!"

"Why would I do that? Your Majesty is obviously exhausted and doesn't wish my company. Besides I take up too much room."

His eyes took on a new light when her hands moved down to her belly. As if caught in the throes of an intense emotion, he winced.

"Sit on me. Now!"

"Hold on a second, let me get this straight. Is your Majesty begging me to sit on him?"

The way he flexed his hands told Liv their first encounter was bright and vivid in his mind. As if recalling the sexual scene increased his desire, his wince deepened.

"Sit on me."

Like a goddess of love, she didn't make a move towards him but slid her hand down between her legs, entangling her fingers in the curls of her bush. And something incredible happened. Chastened, the king of the Overworld closed his eyes to utter a single word.

"Please."

Placing her legs on each side of his body, she got hold of his outstretched arms to lower herself down on him. When her sex brushed his erection, his eyes flew open. A fierce expression of desire crossed his features and she gave him an order.

"Don't move."

Keeping a firm grip on his forearms, she sucked in his hard cock. Faces inches apart, gazes melting into each other's, they both moaned. While she took him all the way in, the tight muscles of his arms rolled under her fingers. She moistened her lips with her tongue, and exhaled as his dick rubbed the whole length of her cunt and charged her up with power.

She was on top. By defying him she had ensured a dominant position. What she hadn't exactly planned was her own longing for penetration, the abrupt craving that burned her mind and demanded more — begged her to gobble up his long, steely sex. To swallow it into her deepest folds, to tremble as it expanded in her, and to drive it relentlessly to fulfilment.

Up and down she went, their flesh coupling, their sighs pairing to fill the room with passion. She had never made love this intensely before, never would have imagined the wondrous feel of his stiff rod so deep inside her. The erotic position they held magnified her lust, but staring into his mesmerising gaze while devouring his cock brought tears to her eyes.

She wanted to kiss him so much that she sat on him to lean forward. But as soon as her grip on his arms slackened, he circled her waist with his hands. Even if he enjoyed being taken care of, he obviously had something else in mind.

"My turn, kitten."

Delighted groans broke loose when he lifted her up to draw his erect dick out of her constricted sex. While he rose to his knees, he placed one of his hands on the small of her back, and urged her to lie back.

Floating on the water, nipples pointing straight to the ceiling, hair dangling down towards the bottom of the tub, she let him turn off the gurgling bubbles. The sudden silence aroused her even more. Attuned to the gentle push of his hands, she spread her legs.

"Use the handles behind you."

She reached out, her hands quickly touching the cold handles. She took hold of them while he positioned himself between her open legs. The need to be penetrated almost felt too much to bear. She clutched the handles tighter as he placed the back of her thighs on his shoulders. With a slow caress, he slid his hands under her buttocks to lift her body above the waterline. There was no mistaking his next move.

Neither of them had forgotten their first encounter. His handsome face inches from her drenched slit, he glanced up. When his direct gaze met hers she read how she turned him on so much all he wanted was to please her. No begging there. No order. Just genuine desire conveyed by his fervent look and his heightened tone of voice.

"Let me love you."

She nodded. The sight of his illuminated eyes made her heart vibrate with passion. She might have basked in his golden stare forever had he not dipped his nose down.

Then she had to squeeze her fingers tightly around the handles as he sucked her lips in his mouth. Unable to quell a long moan although he barely touched her, she realised at once he had the power to make her come any time he wanted. Did she enjoy this idea? Oh yes, she did.

Her body aware of his tiniest movement, she moaned again when he inserted his tongue between her folds to explore a little more of her. Unbroken shards of pleasure reverberating through her limbs, she whimpered like an animal. And she felt the birth of a violent orgasm.

"This is too much, I won't resist..."

The soft touch of his mouth left her as he raised his head to look at her erect breasts, at the expression on her face. He smiled then, the sincere gesture drilling her heart.

"Hush, kitten. Close your eyes and let me love you."

She did just that. This time he licked one of her inner lips from one end to the other. Moving on to her other lip, he nibbled it with agonising slowness before pinching it between his teeth.

She let out a cry, a deep sensation igniting in the pit of her stomach to travel to her overexcited pussy. He sucked her into his mouth and thrust his tongue between her lips as if he felt the strong emotion running through her body. Her arms and legs quivered. Shaking with tremors, she bit her lip to refrain from yelling.

Her whole body strained from the delight of his ravenous touch. He kept a tight hold on her ass to steady her. Hands firm around her buttocks he leisurely moved his tongue inside her hot sheath, licking the offered flesh, sucking her from the inside out. The lingering sensation of wild pleasure that had grabbed her by the guts shot up to a new level, and she braced herself.

As he lapped quicker, she cried out. Her shout stopped him. He retreated and the abrupt departure of his mouth caused her to open her eyes in a rush.

Stiffening her spine to look at him, she wondered if he thought he had hurt her in any way. So when his face appeared in her field of vision, her heart missed a beat. And when he spoke, her pulse raced.

"You're about to come, aren't you?"

Although desire and excitement were written on his features, she briefly toyed with the idea of him frustrating her again. As much as she wished to trust him and believe in him, he remained unpredictable. Then she saw the glimmer in his eyes, the peculiar glint that told her what she craved to know. He didn't mean to frustrate her. He wanted to become unforgettable.

As the realisation hit her, her eyes widened. With a slight move, he pulled her buttocks apart before dipping his head down. A single lick on her breached pussy and the smouldering fire in her blazed high.

Resting her head back against the ledge of the tub, feeling heat coming off the handles she gripped like an anchor, she shuddered in anticipation. But the licking had ceased and his next words seemed to caress her ears.

"Hold it for me. Hold it until I say otherwise because I want you to come like you never have."

She listened to him. She contracted her muscles when he kissed her belly button, his tongue inflaming her skin from navel to pubic hair. But when he closed his mouth around her throbbing sex, an irresistible surge rushed to the surface and threatened to explode. He stilled. Focused on holding off her orgasm, she gasped hard.

"I can't…"

The raging fire seemed to feed on her every nerve, to become alive from the simple pressure of his lips. She saw streaks of light behind her closed eyelids and thought she'd pass out.

"Yes, you can, just a little longer. Do it for me."

He had talked and she hadn't yet registered that he wasn't touching her anymore. The heated metal of the handles appeared to stick to her palms. She clutched them tighter, her nails digging into her skin. But she didn't feel the slightest pain, her mind riveted, fastened to the inferno seething between her thighs.

Then he blew into her cunt. She writhed in his strong grasp, blurting out high-pitched wails that sliced through the quiet room. She trembled so violently she felt his hands leave her buttocks to circle her waist. Her insides ablaze, her ragged breath singing her lungs, she panted.

"Please, please, I can't wait anymore."

"I know, kitten. I'm gonna touch you now, and I want you to burst in my mouth."

His much-needed words almost propelled her over the brink. Teeth gritted, she arched her back, belly rising, pussy in line with his mouth and tongue. All her muscles locked in expectation of his final move she squeezed her lips when he didn't touch her.

Her clitoris kept throbbing, her whole body shuddering from an inner tension she wouldn't be able to repress a second longer. For the love of God, what was he waiting for? Yet she held in the forceful heat now irradiating her flesh to the point where she thought she'd lose her mind.

Apart from his hands around her waist, she couldn't feel him or hear him. Why wasn't he touching her? Why? And just as her delirious pussy gave up on waiting for him, his tongue penetrated her. Hard and sleek, it shot up her cunt like a rocket.

Chapter Twenty-Six

The world burst into glittering pieces. A liberating scream whooshed up her throat as her juices poured out into his mouth. Her legs and arms thrashed uncontrollably, splashing water on her face and breasts. Dying from sheer pleasure she kicked, but he bore her convulsing body while he suckled the sweetness of her excruciating release.

Then she did pass out. A brief black-out, a few seconds of consciousness robbed from her. When she opened her eyes and raised her head, her body floated on the warm water, suffused with an incredible sensation of completion. She wasn't holding the handles anymore, but her spread-out arms also appeared to be floating. She felt whole, satisfied beyond imagining and completely in love with the vampire above her.

Bent over hers, his face showed traces of concern. Did he think she would actually die from pleasure? As she focused on the sensual curve of his lips he smiled. And this time the king of the Overworld didn't look smug. He looked elated.

"Welcome back, little girl. You had me there for a while. Here, sit down a minute."

Hands on her shoulders, he guided her down until her butt came in contact with the bottom of the tub. Her eyes never left his face. This man had just given her unbelievable pleasure, yet while he now gently fussed over her he touched her very core — the vulnerable soul she bared to him. Almost as if sensing her pure emotion, he raised an eyebrow.

"Happy?"

Happy was a feeble word. Ravished out of her mind would have been more like it. Swallowing to cool her dry throat, she exhaled. Her long sigh brought a new grin to his face. Beyond looking elated, his features also showed an expression of longing she had come across on several occasions.

Overwhelmed by her body's reactions, she had forgotten about him. She glanced down. He was sitting on his heels and, at once, her eyes caught sight of his erect cock pointed at her, of the width of his rod enlarged by the clear water separating them. She might have stared at it for a long time had he not broken the silence.

"I'm sorry. Watching you come has been a very exciting experience. I just need a little time to cool off."

She couldn't believe her ears. The monarch of all vampires was apologising because she had turned him on? Although well aware he had satisfied her needs, he seemed prepared to brush aside his own pleasure — to let her rest, to give her freedom. Holy mackerel, how had their complicated relationship been turned around like this?

Of course he had drained her energy, but the fierce desire in his eyes had her pulse quickening. Like a serpent awakening from a shallow slumber the vibe stirred in her stomach. Guided by instinct as much as renewed lust, she sat up straight and reached out.

"What are you doing?"

In spite of his decision to turn a blind eye on lovemaking, his voice sounded rougher than usual and he didn't seem able to take his eyes off her hand, halfway between them.

"Hush, your Majesty. Close your eyes."

He did. And he sighed when she encircled the base of his dick, her fingers coiling around the solid member. He felt so stiff in her hand that the inner vibration lurched. He moaned when she stretched the skin upward, and a sudden wave of heat tickled her pussy.

Surprised at her own readiness, she began masturbating him. Her fingers moving up and down, alternately clenching and relaxing, she loved the way it felt. She didn't go fast. She just relished the thought of giving him pleasure while she watched his reactions. He winced every time she brushed the crown of his dick with her fingers. He bit his lip and moaned when she picked up speed to increase his growing excitement.

The hardness of his cock in her hand brought back the full desire he had momentarily appeased. The opportunity to watch at leisure his beautiful face had her wet in less than a minute. The more she caressed him, the more insistent the vibe became.

Without letting go of him, she brought her free hand forward. Fingers splayed out, she began rolling his dick between her palms. Liv's breathing quickened and hairs rose on the nape of her neck when he groaned.

Why was she only discovering now the gratification of giving a hand job? His usually smooth brow lined in unison with the movements of her palms, his eyelids twitching from enjoyment, his full lips parted to release ragged breaths, the skin on his knuckles stretched white because he was gripping the ledge of the tub like a maniac. Even if she lived to be a hundred this memory would be carved in her mind.

In awe of the sexual influence she had on the mighty vampire king kneeling before her, she removed her left hand to enclose the top half of his cock with her right hand. Fingers firm but gentle, she concentrated her rubbing on his sensitive crown.

He uttered a sharp grunt. Brow creased, lips pressed together, he looked on the verge of losing control. A ripple coursed through him from the tendons of his neck down to the base of his fingernails. His pecs flexed and hardened, sticking out like iron squares. His biceps bulged, contracting the muscles of his forearms.

On both sides of her, she heard a cracking noise as his clawed fingers dug into the now deformed ledge. Watching him, a sense of wonder filled her at the thought of the power she held in her hands. The power she held over him. But something else caught her attention.

Open-mouthed, she watched his features shift. She stroked the tip of his cock and the skin over his cheekbones appeared to strain while his face acquired a radiant golden shade. She masturbated him a fraction faster and watched with delight two long fangs appearing out of his mouth. When his elongated eyes flew open, the freckles seemed to swim in the surrounding darkness.

With his intense gaze boring into hers, devouring her, she became a shrine of desire. Placing one of his hands around hers to halt her movements he licked his fangs with his tongue.

"I want to be inside you. I need to feel your tight little cunt wrapped around my cock. I'm so hard for you."

Her heart lurched. Her clitoris throbbed. The muscles in her pussy quivered. Letting go of his rigid sex, she started at the abrupt hammering of her heart when he cocked his head towards the handles behind her.

Reminded of the tremendous orgasm she had already experienced, a fierce jag of excitement ran down her spine when the term 'handles' crossed her mind. Lying back, she grasped them while he moved between her open thighs, his erection aimed at her hole.

When his tip touched her, tremors of anticipation made her shiver. When he breached her, the forceful sensation of his unyielding cock shook her whole body. In unison, his hands contracted around her waist as he uttered, "Hell, this feels so fucking good!"

She couldn't have found a better way to put it. As he began going in and out of her vibrating hot sheath, her mind relinquished all control and her emotions took charge. His deep thrusts affecting her very core, she became a ball of flame in his hands.

Unable to take her eyes off his striking vampiric features, she stopped blinking. His rigid dick kneading her damp flesh, the thought of making love to him for the rest of her life hit her. To top it all, the idea of spending her days and nights by his side excited her even more. His words hit home when he cursed.

"Fuck! You're so damn hot I could make love to you forever."

Her body contracted as he slightly shifted to shove his sex deeper into her. With each thrust his cock grazed her feverish clit. With each thump he gave her a pound of his love.

She heard her own cries blended with his raw grunts of pleasure, as if from far away. Just as the vibe began meshing with a surge of wild sensations rising from her loins, she perceived a decrease in his physical intensity. Like stars twinkling in the night sky, the freckles in his eyes seemed to caress her face and his ragged voice penetrated her bubble of happiness.

"Hang on, kitten!"

"Why?"

Without waiting for an answer, she had already tightened her hold on the handles.

"Because you're in for a hell of a ride, baby."

She felt his firm grip on her hips, a second of hesitation, and her world exploded with mind-numbing pleasure. Consumed from the inside out like a living torch, she writhed in his hands, her body thrashing about, her heart reeling, her spirit submerged in the realms of an inconceivable orgasm. And as a torturing bliss conquered her, she heard his blissful outcry just before words of love flowed out of her mouth. Her love for him.

Time lost reality. Reality lost meaning. Like a feather gliding down from the vault of heaven, she came back to her senses. When she opened her eyes, he was licking the spot on her neck where he had bitten her. He raised his head and a mellow sensation infused her with love. Eyes elongated, skin colour matching the precious stars in his gaze, he regarded her.

"You love me?"

His tone only conveyed sobriety and something else that she didn't dare call hope. Although his question sounded genuine, she had been treated offhandedly too often to acknowledge it out loud just yet.

She blinked. Looking around she realised she was sitting in the tub again, not holding the handles anymore. He knelt between her spread legs, and she hadn't even felt him come out of her.

"What happened? I mean, what was that?"

He stroked the bite on her neck one last time before straightening up. Raising an eyebrow, he grinned.

"High-speed vampire love."

Eyes wide, she stared at him until he took her in his arms and stood her up on her feet. Naked, he strode to the closet to bring back two bath towels. Then he enveloped her shivering body before resuming.

"You know... In and out, but vampire speed. Too fast for a human eye to perceive, yet very intense."

"Intense is a weak word to describe it."

"Does it mean I pleased you, kitten?"

She stepped out of the tub to dry herself off. When she didn't answer his question, he let his towel fall to the floor to cup her face in his hands, his smile warming her heart.

"I will take your silence as a yes."

Then he picked up his towel and began rubbing his dark hair. By the time Liv felt dry enough to put the black robe on, Raskhan looked human again and he was fully dressed. He escorted her to the door before leading the way towards what she assumed would be her bedroom. As it happened they never reached their intended destination.

They were following an open gallery situated on a higher level above the main hallway when shouts broke out. Raskhan stopped walking to lean over the railing. A tall statue obstructing her view, Liv stepped aside to get a drift of what the sudden commotion was about.

For the first time since she had set foot in the Overworld, she witnessed a gathering of vampires and a disturbance in their quiet, routine activity. Downstairs, a crowd had assembled around one man. Right by her side, Raskhan sighed deeply.

Twisting her head, Liv finally caught a glimpse of the newcomer, and her heart stuttered. Rogan was back.

Chapter Twenty-Seven

He lay unconscious in the arms of two vampires carrying him. Before Liv could blink, the crowd had spread out a little, and Raskhan already stood beside Rogan. A hush fell over the grand hallway. All staring at the king of the Overworld, they awaited his orders.

"Zontag!"

The older vampire came forward. Bending over Rogan, he lifted his stained white shirt to reveal his side. What he saw there mustn't have agreed with him because he looked at the king and shook his head.

"He's in very bad shape. I'll see what I can do for him, but it's a wonder he's still alive."

As he let go of the shirt, Zontag seemed to be unable to stop shaking his head. On the other side of Rogan's body, the king didn't waste his breath with small talk, but snapped his fingers.

"He is of royal blood. Have a cremation ceremony arranged."

What? What was he saying? He couldn't let his brother die without at least trying to save him. Did Raskhan hate him that much? Would he be happy with Rogan dead? Yet, just like that, the captivating Raskhan who had shown her the meaning of the word ecstasy had vanished, and the cruel, authoritative king had reappeared.

Clutching the railing until her knuckles whitened, Liv ignored a sudden bitter taste in her mouth. Heart heavy, she swallowed her blooming hopes and desires while Rogan's body was carried away, and Raskhan took off in the opposite direction. Most of all, she wondered if she had it in her to love someone who rejoiced in his brother's death.

She stood for painful seconds. The vibe beat for Raskhan and Raskhan alone, loud and clear inside her. Not so loud and not so clear, her feelings for Rogan made her want to cower down. Her mind ripped with guilt, she forced herself to breathe evenly.

She had betrayed him. He had confessed his love for her, he had asked her to wait for him and she had run into his brother's arms. Hold on, that wasn't exactly true. In her defence, the first time with Raskhan she had been misled into thinking he was Rogan.

But what of the other times she had raved with passion under Raskhan's blazing touch? She knew by then. She had offered her body and heart to the king of the Overworld with full knowledge of the facts. In her book this was betrayal.

Liv winced with pain when she loosened her tight grip on the railing. She watched the carriers climb up the stairs leading onto the first floor landing. She needed to see where they were taking Rogan. Her Rogan—the cherished vampire who had saved her life. The man she had professed to love it seemed a lifetime ago.

As they mounted the steps, Liv crouched and hid behind the statue. Invisible from below, she felt like a mouse in a lion's den. From the direction they were going she gathered Rogan would end up in the room she had exited moments ago. Of course, it must be the only place with a table long enough to accommodate an unconscious body. Ironically it was also the room where Raskhan had just made blinding love to her.

Assuming her guess was right she stood up and started walking away from them. Raskhan might spot her but hiding behind a statue was pointless. And as much as she wanted to she couldn't follow Rogan. Not yet.

Liv reached her bedroom without anyone halting her. Inside, Zontag sat on the bed, waiting. A small, sad smile creased his features when she came in the room.

Apart from the royal twin brothers, he was the only familiar face. For some reason Liv had trusted him on sight, even when he had taken fluids out of her. Did he remind her of a father figure? Tears wetting her cheeks, she sat by him and choked on her tears when he held her hand.

"I'm sorry you had to see that."

"Is he really dying?"

"I'm afraid he is. There's nothing I can do for him. If I had the skills to save him, I promise you I would."

Vision blurred, she smiled at him. Here was an immortal willing to defy his king to save another, and she believed him. Opening the handbag she had left on the bed earlier, Liv took out some paper tissues. She wiped her cheeks before blowing her nose.

"Does Raskhan know you're here with me?"

"He sent me. He thought you might need a shoulder to cry on."

She snorted. Her mouth twisted in a disappointed, bitter scorn, she looked at Zontag straight in the eye.

"Oh, yeah, as if he cared! He just killed his brother, for crying out loud! What does he expect from me? Sympathy? Understanding? Forgiveness, maybe? Well, let me tell you something, Zontag. As far as I'm concerned, your high and mighty king can go to hell!"

Unfazed by her outburst, Zontag patted her hand. "Hush, my dear, walls have ears around here."

"I don't give a shit if he can hear me or not, and I'd gladly repeat it to his face. He had no right to do that."

"You know, Raskhan didn't kill Rogan. Khord did. With the help of his hunters' team, he finally located Rogan in your world."

Khord again. That freakish bastard must have been delighted to act on his king's orders. He should be rotting in hell, but instead he might well be promoted for his undying loyalty. She felt like screaming from frustration, but just then Zontag did something strange.

Raising a finger to his lips to indicate some kind of secret, he shook a clean tissue open and brought it to her face. Trusting her instincts, Liv took the offering to apply it on her face. When he nodded she uttered whiny noises, and made a great show of blowing her empty nose.

Meanwhile Zontag used the crossword book and the pen lying on the bed. She watched him scribble something on a page. As he raised the book in front of her eyes, she feigned a bout of coughing—but when she read the words, her coughing turned real.

Rogan has been shot with a silver bullet. You can save him.

A wild hope surged from the darkness of her despair. She cleared her throat as the older vampire got up.

"Let me fetch you some water."

While he walked to the bathroom, she reread the magic words. Rogan was dying, but she possessed the power to save him. She had done it before, she could do it again. Forgetting all about her misery, she looked at Zontag with a brilliant smile as he handed her a glass of water.

"Thank you."

Liv took a sip, fresh water cooling her irritated throat. When she saw Zontag reaching for the book again, she made sure to drink the whole glass with a lot of noise. Still, the silence between them was lengthening, and if walls had ears one of them should speak.

"Can I see Rogan?"

"I'm afraid not. You are to stay in his room, king's orders."

"His room?"

"Yes, this is Rogan's bedroom. Didn't you know?"

Definitely the worst trick Raskhan had played on her. Fully aware she'd find out at some point, he had chosen to let her stay in his brother's bedroom. As a vivid reminder of Rogan's absence? To torture her? To fuck her in his brother's bed? Dear God, what a bastard!

As the lump in her throat hardened to the size of a small stone, Zontag held out the crossword book for her. She grabbed it with renewed strength, her heart going haywire. To give her some time to read it, Zontag launched into a clever monologue ranging from "I know this has been shocking news but..." to reassuring sentences like "Don't worry, you'll feel better soon." Listening with only one ear, Liv read his neat handwriting.

Ask for some food. Take your time to eat while I'll be doing everything I can to clear the way for you. Rogan is in the spa room. Be quick and discreet.

She closed her book to give him the thumbs up. Playing her part, she snivelled loudly before cutting him short.

"Listen, Zontag, I appreciate what you're trying to do but, if you don't mind, I'd rather be alone for a while."

"I understand. I'll check on you later."

He stood up and squeezed her hand a final time, his blue gaze conveying an expression that could only be translated as 'Good luck!' Taking a deep breath, Liv waited for him to reach the bedroom door before acting on the instructions he had given her.

"By the way, Zontag, do you think I could get some food? I'm beginning to feel hungry."

"Sure. I'll have something sent to you very shortly."

"Thanks."

"Have some rest now."

She waved at him before he disappeared into the hallway, feeling like a little girl about to embark on a mysterious voyage. But this was no game. Now that the council knew she hadn't committed a crime of lese-majesty, her death sentence had to be null and void. Yet, somehow, she believed it wouldn't change their minds about her being a deadly threat to their race.

True to his word, Zontag proved very efficient. Less than five minutes later a servant brought her an aromatic paper bag. As usual in this place, he left her room without delay. Although her hopes had soared, the greasy smell wafting from the bag didn't appeal to her.

She couldn't eat while Rogan was dying. Glancing up, she observed what she now knew to be his bedroom. Not huge, but comfortable. Not a king's room. Her gaze coming to rest on the writing desk, she then figured out why she had found the book of ancient prophecies lying in the drawer.

She had believed her discovery convenient and once more she had been so wrong. The manuscript hadn't been stashed there on her account, but it was in its rightful place. Rogan's book. Rogan's bedroom. And in a deep corner of her mind, she pictured a sly smile on Raskhan's face.

Angry at herself for not understanding sooner, Liv retrieved the small hairbrush she kept in her purse for emergencies. Grooming relaxed her frayed nerves as she attempted to give her hair a semblance of order. If she succeeded in saving Rogan she wanted to look good for him.

And what about Raskhan? Did she want to be beautiful for him? No, she wouldn't think of the king. Although the thought of him tugged at her heartstrings, she forced it back. Too hurtful to dwell on it now.

When she felt confident that enough time had elapsed, Liv opened her bedroom door with as much stealth as she could muster. Adrenaline jabbing her muscles, she stepped out and checked both ways.

The hallway appeared empty. Praying to God to let her accomplish her mission, she moved furtively to the end of the corridor—and stopped dead in her tracks. Too late she felt the vibe stir within her stomach. Way too late she heard his ice-cold voice right behind her.

"Where are you going?"

Chapter Twenty-Eight

He must have used his vampire speed to sneak up on her, and the vibration hadn't had enough time to warn her. Wheeling round, Liv raised her gaze to the king's impassive face. The amusement and playfulness he had shown in the spa room had been eradicated with Rogan's return.

"I was looking for you."

"What for?"

Although she didn't enjoy lying, she'd have to suck it up for Rogan's sake. Her mind faster than a racing car, she grasped at the first plausible excuse.

"I wanna go home."

"I forbid it."

He crossed his arms over his chest. Dressed in black from head to toe, he did look like a beautiful angel of death. If going home had been her real intention, she wouldn't have swayed him one jot. As things stood, she simply needed him to believe her.

"Why not? What's it to you, anyway? What do you care?"

"I have my reasons."

"Oh, yeah, like what? Do you want me here to satisfy your lust? Do you really think I could let you touch me now that you've had Rogan killed? For Christ's sake, he's your brother!"

Liv had started out meaning to deceive him, but, to her surprise genuine, let-down and resentment tumbled out of her mouth. Even the sight of his icy stare and knitted lips couldn't stop her.

"Damn the day you trespassed on my life. I could have..." She trailed off to inhale loudly. "I could have had feelings for you, but you've ruined everything. You're not a king to me. You're just a petty, lousy murderer, and Rogan is way out of your league."

She gasped for air. Just as she thought she was getting her breath back, he pinned her to the wall. He towered over her and his voice took on a biting, raw undertone she had never heard before.

"If I want your opinion, I will ask for it. In the meantime I suggest you shut the fuck up, and run the hell back to your room."

Unable to move a single muscle, frozen by his frigid eyes, she stared at him. Then a shrilling fire alarm pierced her ears, and he released her. Glancing back the way he had come, he cursed as shouts of "Fire!" erupted downstairs.

"What the fuck is going on now?"

With that, he was gone. Putting her hands over her ears, Liv hesitated, but only for a second. She would run all right, just not back to her room. Could it be Zontag creating a diversion? In any case, it was now or never. Disregarding her intricate, confusing feelings for Raskhan, she gritted her teeth in order to bear the painful wail of the siren, and flew in the opposite direction. This was her chance to get to Rogan, and the diversion wouldn't last forever.

She dashed straight to the spa without encountering a single vampire. They must have all gathered downstairs to fight off the fire, and she wished they'd all burn to ashes. Vampires bad, fire good!

She bolted towards the room. Without bothering to check her surroundings, she let herself in. As she closed the door behind her, the shrieking wail diminished.

Rogan lay on a massage table, motionless. Liv approached him slowly. Both hands on her mouth, she started at the sight of his hollowed face. Complexion deathly pale, sunken cheeks, dark rings under his eyes, he was dying all right.

But, in spite of his ghastly appearance, he was *her* Rogan and he was gorgeous. Although time might be running out, she couldn't help but observe him. So like Raskhan. Yet the term 'like' didn't begin to compare them. They didn't share likeness, they shared sameness. For the life of her, she wondered how they could be so different inside.

Outside the room the wailing of the fire alarm lessened, urging her to get a move on. With great care she lifted Rogan's shirt where a large bloody stain indicated the wound. Like the first time he had been shot, the silver bullet had gone straight through his body and left a gaping hole.

Liv applied her right hand to the entrance wound. Closing her eyes, she willed herself to shut out the disturbing siren outside and concentrate on healing his broken body. A slight inner tingle raised goose bumps on her arms, but not much else. *Come on!* She had to do this right.

Drawing in a long breath, she recalled the first time Rogan had kissed her. In her living room, both of them attracted to the other like magnets, she had felt so nervous then. But his long kiss had tasted like a sliver of heaven. Now she felt furiously glad Raskhan had never kissed her.

Lost in tender recollections, Liv almost jumped in surprise when the force brutally lashed out. She felt an incredible power storm out of her being to crash into the dying vampire, and invade his whole body. Caught unaware by its startling emergence and intenseness, she almost cried out when the flaming tongue leapt from one to the other.

Without knowing why, she perceived the healing sensations to be different this time—quicker and stronger. Perhaps she was getting better at the job. She didn't feel as tired.

Her heart beating like a wild sparrow, she looked at Rogan. His features still appeared hollowed and devoid of life, but when she withdrew her hands the gaping hole had been filled. Letting out a relieved sigh, Liv touched the perfect, healthy-looking skin to make sure she wasn't dreaming. But no, she had done it. She had healed Rogan again.

A smile of pure happiness lifting the corners of her mouth, she felt like dancing right there between the hot tub and the massage table. Except that she suddenly realised that the screeching fire alarm couldn't be heard anymore. How long ago had it stopped?

As much as she wanted to stay with Rogan until he woke up, the idea sounded bad. He might come to in a few minutes or hours and she didn't have that much time to spare. Whether the vampires had managed to put the fire out or had found out there wasn't any fire in the first place, they'd come to check on Rogan. And Raskhan would definitely look for her.

Her eyes watering from joy, Liv passed a gentle hand across his forehead. Although he didn't stir, she knew in her heart he was going to be fine. He just needed a little time.

With a last glance at the unconscious man, she retreated to the door. On leaving, she activated the lever she had seen Raskhan use. Soundlessly, the panel covering the two-way mirror slid open. She might well not be able to stay with Rogan, but she would watch him come back to life.

She ran again. Retracing her steps, Liv raced along the back ways straight to Zontag's lab all the while praying not to be spotted. She barged into the lab, a little breathless but delighted to have made it without problems. Dear God, she had never run so much since her teenage years.

Looking around to ensure she was alone, she went to the older vampire's worktable. She found the button in a matter of seconds, and pressed it. On the back wall of the lab, the two-way mirror slid open. Excited beyond reasonable measure, she approached it slowly.

Even from there she could tell a change had already taken place. Still unconscious, Rogan nonetheless looked much better. Cheeks fuller, he didn't seem as pale as he had been a minute ago. As Liv watched, his whole body shuddered. Yet he didn't open his eyes.

Waiting being her only option, she waited. She had quit biting her nails when she had turned eighteen, but the long-lost compulsion suddenly rose up. To nip it in the bud, she placed her hands on the thick window. As if she possessed a magic touch, Rogan moved.

Not much at first—just an indistinct stretching of limbs, a vague sense of consciousness returning.

Unable to remove her hands from the mirror, Liv studied the smallest of his movements. Pretty soon, his hands twitched. Holding her breath, she felt her heart kick when his eyes popped open.

Motionless, he stared at the ceiling for what seemed like hours, but must have been seconds. Although Liv stood too far away to see them, she knew the golden freckles were lively in his dark gaze. As if in slow motion, Rogan rested his elbows closer to his sides, swung his legs over the massage table, and pushed himself into a sitting position.

He stayed there for a while before standing up. Testing his strength he crossed the room away from the door and towards her, but his eyes only passed over the two-way mirror. While he rolled his shoulders and stretched his neck, a familiar sensation woke up in Liv's stomach. The vibe.

She began to panic as the soft fluttering roused from sleep, but quickly understood the feeling wasn't increasing. Raskhan must be close by, yet some distance away. With that also came the painful realisation that she had just spent long minutes with Rogan, touching Rogan, without ever feeling the vibe. Why did it have to be Raskhan?

On the other side of the mirror, Rogan suddenly turned round to face the door. Body tensed, Liv looked at the door too. As it swung open to make way for the king of the Overworld, she let out a soundless breath.

A tall shadow of darkness, Raskhan stared at his brother. The white shirt tainted with his own blood and enhancing his pale features, Rogan stared at his brother. Cliché as it was, the image of a demon and an angel fighting to the death seized Liv's mind. Her heart knocking hard, she felt riveted to the two vampires who had rocked her world.

The standstill didn't last long. As the door clicked shut, Raskhan and Rogan rushed into each other's arms and hugged like brothers.

Chapter Twenty-Nine

Liv rubbed her eyes. Could she have fallen asleep and started dreaming? Had she been transported to another planet without her knowledge? Had her last meal been spiked with magic mushrooms? She blinked a few times, but on the other side of the mirror the twins were still hugging and clapping each other's backs. Holy mackerel, she hadn't seen this one coming!

Hands pinned to the window, mouth agape, she watched the fraternal reunion. A violent surge of happiness shook her at the vision of their beaming smiles as they finally took a step away from each other. Now clasping hands and forearms, they both looked overjoyed.

Then they started talking, but she couldn't hear a single word. For once, she wished she had taken a course in lip-reading. That would have been extremely useful right now. Whatever they were saying, they kept smiling at each other. At some point, Rogan threw his head back and laughed.

There was no point in hiding in the lab. Curiosity gnawing at her, Liv went to close the two-way mirror before walking to the door. She needed to know what the heck was going on. She deserved a clear explanation about the so-called hatred fuelling them, and she would get it now. As she stepped out of the lab, a rough hand clamped her mouth.

"Hey, slut, looks like you and me are going on a little trip."

Then she experienced a blur of movement, a whooshing sound in her ears, and cold air slapped her face. When the world stopped moving, she brought her hands to her belly to quiet a slight nauseating sensation. Then she blinked to make sense of what stood in lieu of the lab door.

The deepest night engulfed her in an oppressive embrace. She had to let her eyes adjust to the sudden darkness to understand the new landscape. She only saw emptiness all around except in front of her where black buildings formed the edge of town. But, with some light coming off them, she was able to see enough to realise the danger of her position.

Straight on, at least a mile away, she spotted the white marble reflection of the king's palace. She was on the border of an endless desert, and Khord was standing beside her.

"Ha, ha, I got you this time, didn't I?"

The ugly brute must have used his vampire speed to career her out of the palace and far into this cold, infinite night. Liv concealed the wall of fear constricting her guts as best as she could.

"Oh, yeah, and the king is gonna get you now!"

"He's too busy ensuring his brother is dying. Besides, he doesn't give a shit about what you do or don't do." Spit on his mouth, Khord uttered a rough bark of laughter. "Oh, don't tell me you thought he'd fall for you like Rogan did. Hell, this is so hilarious!"

"You disgust me!"

Shrugging, Liv started walking towards the faraway palace. She gasped when Khord grabbed her arm and threw her onto the ground. Pain shot up her knee, but she barely felt it as the monster loomed over her and ripped apart the bottom half of her black robe.

"Such a pity lover boy will never know about this."

He wanted to rape her, and she couldn't push the fear away, the wild terror now running free in her veins. Eyes wide, Liv caught some movement to her left. So afraid to look away from Khord she nevertheless glanced sideways. Tall and menacing, three vampires watched them.

Recognising the hungry look burning in their eyes, Liv realised she wouldn't get out of this alive. Her body seeming to weigh a ton, a terrible dread keeping her flat on the dusty ground, her throat too tight to scream, she felt panic work its way inside her. Khord twisted his lips.

"Hey, you slut, don't look so terrified. How about a smile to greet my friends? They're rogue vampires, and, trust me, they'd love a taste of you. They haven't fed off a human in a long time."

What kind of Bringer of Death was she? The 'quitting when things got a little rough' kind? If she possessed an ounce of courage and determination, she should get up and fight for her life. Unfortunately, all she had going for her was a sensible awareness of her position.

In the best-case scenario she might be able to turn Khord into a human. Providing her power worked, then what? Even as a man he would still be much stronger than her, and the three other vampires wouldn't waste time to pounce on her. No way out. No option.

Trapped in a no-win situation, Liv shut her eyes when Khord's large body fell on her. She winced from pain, but held on to the single image filling her mind — Raskhan taking her into the safety of his arms. Raskhan's passionate gaze boring into hers as he made love to her.

There she had it. About to be raped and probably torn to pieces, there could be no lying to herself, no deceiving, no denying the truth or the depth of her feelings — she loved the king of the Overworld.

Yet the horror writhing in her blood escalated when Khord's hands gripped her bare thighs, his fingers squeezing her flesh so hard her eyes watered. As if his revolting touch liberated her pent-up throat, her eyes flew open and she screamed her lungs out. His horrid face right above her, she put her hands on his shoulders to push him back.

He was hurled from her as if a giant, invisible force heaved his body. He crashed on the ground at least ten feet away with a thumping, cracking noise, clouds of dust swirling around him.

Before Liv could wonder about her unexpected new strength, Raskhan was on his knees beside her. Lifting her up, he carried her to the first black building behind them. Shaken but oh so relieved to be alive, she leaned against the cold wall as he cupped her face in his hands.

"Are you okay?"

She nodded. He was gone in a wink, back to the heart of the battlefield where the three vampires already circled Rogan. Although his white shirt displayed a large bloodstain from the wound she had healed, he looked healthy and more than ready to fight.

Back to back, stakes in hands, standing poised for the first strike, the brothers watched the rogues. From where she stood Liv couldn't tell who'd launched the attack, but her vision suddenly blurred. Only perceiving blunt sounds and vague black shapes colliding, she focused on breathing.

It turned out she didn't possess superhuman strength, but once more Raskhan had saved her from Khord. As Liv's intense fear receded, she began to feel the vibe. Numbed with shock, it now rose slowly inside her belly. The vibe linking her to the king of the Overworld.

The picture seemed to freeze in front of her. Two rogues lay dead on the ground, stakes sticking out of their chests. The third one was up and grabbing Rogan by the throat. Raskhan was nowhere in sight, and the spot where Khord had crashed only showed dust.

With a swift toppling move, Rogan shook off his enemy to ram a stake into his heart. As the rogue dropped dead, a gruesome scream rose up in the distance. Khord or Raskhan? Where were they? Her pulse lurching at the dreadful sound, gooseflesh covering her arms, Liv nonetheless felt reassured when she saw a smile lighting Rogan's face.

Somehow he knew Raskhan was dealing with Khord, and that was good enough for her. Then he turned to her, a beautiful smile still on his lips, his gaze assessing her from head to toe. Whatever had happened since he had left her, she couldn't forget that he had been her Rogan once. On impulse, she ran to him and flung her arms around his neck.

"I'm so glad you're alive."

A surprised look on his face, Rogan gently unlaced her hands from around his neck and took a step back from her.

"I really do appreciate your concern, lovely lady, but who are you?"

Chapter Thirty

Sweet Jesus in heaven, she had healed him wrong. For Rogan not to recognise or remember her only meant she must have healed him wrong. Had he forgotten everything they had shared and suffered? Had she involuntarily erased some parts of his memory when the force invaded his failing body? Holy mackerel, this could not be happening!

Closing her mouth, Liv gaped at him. Rogan let go of her hands with care, and raised a quizzical eyebrow when she didn't answer his question. Like two statues facing each other, they both stared and waited for the other to speak. A fragile silence ensued, soon broken by Raskhan's voice right beside her.

"We're done here. Let's go."

Heedless of his warning tone, Liv slowly twisted her head towards him while she grasped his hand in a gesture of apology. Emotion welling up, she struggled to articulate her distress to Raskhan.

"I'm sorry, but I healed Rogan wrong. Oh, my God, I am so sorry!"

"Hush, kitten, not here. We have to get back to the palace. Khord is still at large, and I don't want to give him another opportunity to hurt you. There, hold on to me now."

However, before Raskhan could take her to safety, shadows moved around them. Coming from behind the closest buildings to the desert, a band of rogues advanced towards the three of them. As they formed a semicircle to block their way to the palace, Liv counted ten vampires.

Ten—way too many for Raskhan and Rogan to defeat them. So outnumbered, even a king couldn't work miracles. Eyes wide, holding her breath, Liv waited for a new swell of fear to override her mind. But as she watched the rogues get into an attacking line, no fear came. And she felt the vibe instead.

Connected to Raskhan, possibly linked to his present emotions, the vibe suddenly infused her with determination, power, and a single relentless goal— kill them all. Was that what he felt? If so, no wonder he had become king. At any rate, she welcomed the potent sensation while she wrenched her gaze away from their enemies to look at him.

He was watching Rogan, but Liv caught the knowing look that passed between the twins. Without any lessons in lip-reading, she also picked up what Raskhan mouthed to his brother.

"Keep her safe."

Without a word, Rogan nodded. She shivered. Did it mean Raskhan was going to die? Would he fight to the death to protect her? Would he give up his life to ensure hers? Did he love her that much?

One of the rogues took a step forward, and it sounded like a clash of titans. They used their inhuman speed to rush at each other, preventing Liv from seeing anything except a vague swirl of black shapes, but the wicked, sticky noises followed by gurgling screams of pain told of hearts impaled on stakes and of blood being spilled. Whose blood?

Although she couldn't make out Raskhan in the moving blur around her, Liv didn't have time to feel helpless. Coming from nowhere, fangs out, a rogue grabbed her head to tilt it to the side. Something that had nothing to do with the vibe raked her from inside. At the same time she heard Raskhan shout her name. Probably overrun with vampires, he couldn't save her this time.

She would. Ignoring the rogue's thirsty grin, she put both her hands on his chest and pushed with her mind. As though anticipating her bidding, the force lashed out. Inches away from her face, the rogue ceased grinning. His eyes took on a faraway look and he released her head. Arms dangling along his sides, mouth agape, appearing disorientated, he shuffled to the edge of the desert and vanished into the darkness.

She had turned him human. Although a victorious sensation endowed her with renewed courage, panic hit her when a wrenching scream echoed from the battle.

Heart pounding, Liv blinked as she caught a clear view of the slaughter. Either exhausted or assessing their chances, they were all back to regular speed. Five rogues lay dead. Half of his face covered in blood but on his feet, Rogan grappled with a vampire. Looking battered yet as resolute as ever, Raskhan fought off two more.

With her attacker clearly out of competition, that left a single rogue missing. But where was he? Disregarding pools of light reflected from the buildings at her back, her eyes scanned the heavy darkness. She sure didn't possess a heightened sense of sight. Being human didn't help in this instance and she needed more light to discern... Her heart lurched.

Raskhan uttered a harsh groan, and fell to his knees. Although quick to pull out the stake protruding from his shoulder, he flew backward when both rogues kicked him square in the chest.

Liv screamed. Focused on the king of the Overworld lying at their feet, they ignored her cry but it distracted Rogan's adversary. This precious second proved fatal. Rogan struck with all his might, the stake piercing flesh, muscles and heart. Even as the vampire collapsed, Rogan jumped on the other two now pinning his brother down.

They tumbled together, rolling on the ground, spraying dust. And Raskhan was up. Eyes elongated, fangs out, crusted blood covering his left shoulder, sleek muscles bulging through his tattered shirt, he looked like the God of Wrath. Rooted to the spot by the sight of his otherworldly, striking features, Liv admired the love of her life.

Weaponless, he rounded on the nearest vampire. Grabbing him by the hair, he pulled him up as if he lifted a puppet. In a heartbeat he seemed to dive into the rogue's neck, tearing flesh, ripping tendons, severing veins. Then he discarded the limp body, and Liv averted her gaze as jets of blood spurted out of a red mass that had once been a throat.

Five feet away, Rogan fought for his life. The remaining vampire sat on top of him, one hand locked around his throat, the other holding a stake. Before Raskhan could help his brother, a black shape hit him full force, and both of them crashed down on the ground.

The missing rogue. The bloodsucker she had looked for a moment ago, but hadn't located. Why had he been hiding? To bide his time? To plan something? She got her answer as a strong arm grabbed her middle from behind and cold metal touched her throat.

"Missed me?"

Body hair stiffening at the sound of the unmistakable, loathed voice, Liv froze. Very aware of the knife on her skin, she followed Khord's lead as he backed her away from the heart of the battle.

She assumed he stopped when he felt a safe distance between them and the combatants. Her back pressed against his body, the blade icing her throat, she saw Raskhan pounce on the remaining rogue. Yet, as he landed on his stomach, he glanced towards her. His eyes widened. Realising she had been taken by Khord, he seemed to lose focus and his enemy drove him back.

"See? You won't be his slut for very long. He won't make it."

Khord's hateful statement rang in her ear. Anger boiling in her veins, she wished she could strangle him. But he held her fast and she had no idea if the force would work without her touching his chest.

"Am I your hostage? Are you going to kill me or do you think you can trade me for your life?"

He had somewhat loosened his grip, but the knife was back against her throat when she finished her sentence.

"Depends on how this ends."

In front of them, neither Raskhan nor Rogan seemed about to gain on their opponents. Former skilled warriors, the rogues now fought with the strength of the desperate. Like a warning alarm, the vibe also told

Liv that Raskhan's fear of losing her didn't play in his favour.

She had to rely on herself, to follow her natural instincts. Thinking fast, she raised a hand towards her stomach to place it on Khord's arm and summoned her sexiest voice.

"Whatever the outcome, don't tell me you don't want a taste of me. I can't believe you wouldn't get what your king had. What Rogan had."

His body stiffened. Seconds stretched, so many that she feared he wouldn't rise to the bait. When he replied at last, a silent breath left her lips.

"Don't try to trick me, bitch. I know you love him, it's written all over your damn face."

"Yes, I love the king..." She paused to carefully slide her free hand behind her back. Open palm facing his pants, she felt her way to his hard crotch. "Whoever the king is."

The brusque harshness of his breath showed she had hit the right spot. Sex and power must have been too difficult to resist for someone like him because he eased the pressure of his arm around her middle to turn her around, and the knife left her throat.

Liv had to stifle a shiver of repulsion when they faced each other. But she could deal with that. As if caressing his body from his groin up, she moved both hands to place them at the centre of his chest. Mustering all her strength, she licked her lips in a sexy fashion.

"So what now, big boy?"

"You didn't fool me like you did the others. Make no mistake, I will teach you what fucking really is."

She felt his hard-on against her belly, she endured the sight of his misshapen teeth and disgusting humid lips, she listened to his exultation of self-satisfaction and victory.

"I knew you were nothing but a horny, greedy bitch. I never believed you were the Bringer of Death."

She slightly cocked her head as she gave the detested warrior her most dazzling smile.

"Well...you should have!"

She pushed so hard a wave of dizziness blinded her for an instant. Fingers flat on his chest, she gasped when the force rose from her core to slam into the warrior. Although he didn't make a sound she knew he'd never threaten her again. Eyes glazed, arms dropping to his sides, a string of saliva flowing from the corner of his mouth, he stared into the distance. The blade clattered to the ground, and Liv collapsed beside it.

Overuse of the force in such a short time had got the better of her. Throwing her hands forward to break her fall, she landed on her front. Though she didn't feel pain she lacked the strength to get back on her feet. Head resting on her forearm, she looked ahead.

In unison, both brothers had their fangs sunk into their opponents' necks. Wrenching bloodied flesh off their throats, they pushed them away and the bodies fell down. Instantly swivelling round, Raskhan looked for her. Fangs red, blood dripping from his mouth, he assessed her situation in a wink. Ignoring a motionless Khord, the king of the Overworld already knelt at her side, wiping his mouth with tatters from his shirt.

"Are you hurt?"

Smiling at the deep concern she read in his eyes, Liv shook her head and lifted her arms. He picked her up, a violent relief shifting his features back to his human face. Glancing aside, he gave a meaningful nod to Rogan.

"Let's go. There might be more rogues around, and we can always retrieve Khord later."

Liv felt a rush of wind on her cheeks, a brief sensation of a world of darkness whizzing past her, and she found herself standing in the centre of the bedroom she occupied in the king's palace. Hard against her body, Raskhan steadied her while Rogan closed the door.

Here, the three of them bathing in the light coming off the walls, Liv got a close look at Rogan. His hair and half of his face drenched in blood, he appeared somewhat aloof and the recollection of what she had done to him lanced her heart. First she had betrayed him then she had healed him wrong.

Her bout of tiredness receding with each passing second, bitters tears rising close to the surface, she watched Raskhan remove the shreds of black fabric from his back while he walked to the bathroom. Water gurgled before he came back to throw a wet towel at his brother.

"Here."

Then he wiped his face and shoulder. Apart from a faint circle, there was no trace of a wound, no evidence he had been stabbed with a stake. Against all odds, the sight of his perfect shoulder amplified Liv's sense of guilt. Raskhan was still perfect, but his brother would never be the same. Because of her.

Overwhelmed by the consequences of her huge blunder, she strained not to cry. Safe in this familiar place, all the fear and pain she had experienced at Khord's hands seemed to flow out of her. But, stronger than relief, an intense need to make Raskhan understand now seized her. He had to know she'd never have harmed Rogan on purpose.

Taking a deep breath, she laced her fingers in prayer. Yet she hesitated, held back by the look on Raskhan's face when he saw her supplicant attitude and the tears in her eyes. Concern lining his brow, he dropped his towel to take hold of her joined hands.

"What is it, kitten?"

"Listen, I have no idea what went wrong when I touched Rogan. Yes, the power came quicker than the first time, but apart from that it felt exactly the same. I promise I didn't mean to heal your brother wrong. I can't control it anyway. Oh, God, what have I done? I'm so sorry!"

Liv quit blubbering when she became aware that Rogan had no clue what she was talking about, and that Raskhan was looking at her with a tender smile. Raising her united hands to his mouth, he kissed the tips of her fingers.

"There's nothing wrong with him. Take it easy now because you healed him just fine."

"No, I didn't. He doesn't remember me."

She might have said more, but Raskhan gently wiped a single tear off her cheek and brushed her lips. Straightening up, he glanced at Rogan who had managed to wash most of the blood off his face. Then he focused on her again. When he spoke, his tone had never sounded so soft.

"Liv, I'd like you to meet my brother...Raskhan."

Chapter Thirty-One

"What?"

If a fatal earthquake had suddenly rattled the whole palace, she wouldn't have felt more thunderstruck. What had he just said? Rogan was Raskhan? Now that was quite simply impossible. She couldn't believe it.

Unless he was testing one of his tricks on her again. Yeah, that sounded much more like the king of the Overworld she had come to love. But he wouldn't have his way so easily this time.

"I see. You're having another good laugh at my expense. Do you really need to involve your brother in this?"

Wiping his fingers with the wet towel, Rogan came up to her and held out his right hand.

"He's telling you the truth. My name is Raskhan, and I'm very pleased to meet you."

Mouth dropping open, Liv automatically shook the proffered hand. Feeling kicked in the guts she shifted her gaze from one brother to the other. No difference. Not a single damn fucking little distinction to tell them apart—and both so strong and handsome.

Raising her hands up as if to ward off demons, she took a step back and let out an astonished "Huh."

At that moment, the vampire she had believed to be Raskhan motioned his brother to leave the room. Once alone he sat her on the edge of the bed, and knelt on the floor at her feet.

"Look at me, kitten."

But she kept her head down, staring at the ripped black robe. He had to lift her chin up before she would meet his eyes. Shiny and golden, the freckles seemed to swim in dark liquid.

"It's me, Rogan. I've never left you. It's been me all along."

"Rogan?"

"Yes, my love."

Something genuine and pleading in his voice finally tore the lack of understanding she was plunged into. With trembling, careful fingers, she touched his cheek.

"I can't believe it."

"Listen to me, and think about it. Since the moment I pretended to be my brother, how many times have you called me Raskhan? How many times have you wished I was Rogan? Don't you remember the night I made love to you as Raskhan and you cried out Rogan's name!"

How could she ever forget that awesome night and his asking for her to love him? Even if their faces sometimes overlapped each other in her mind, she had never stopped thinking of Rogan. And, for a wonder, she suddenly realised she had never called him Raskhan out loud.

"Good point, although it could just have been my way of keeping you alive in my mind."

"Haven't you wondered why I haven't kissed you since you've been in the Overworld? As much as I longed for a kiss, I didn't dare. I was too afraid you'd recognise me."

Holy mackerel, so that was the reason he had frustrated her time and again. But he had been so cruel to her at times, how could she have figured this out? The more he talked, the more she understood that on some deep level she had been deceiving herself. Listening to Rogan, she began to question her judgement. Had she known the truth all along?

"Remember when we said goodbye at the warehouse, I told you I'd find you anywhere because I could feel you inside."

Looking at her intently, Rogan placed one of his hands on her stomach. "Don't you feel me in there? Don't you feel a special vibe between us?"

The damn vibe. From the start she had been convinced it was linked to Raskhan. Because her fear of being alone had been too strong when Rogan had left her at the warehouse, she'd been much too scared to feel it then. And that single instance had completely misled her. Yes, the vibe had always palpitated for Rogan. How else would she have fallen in love with such a rascal?

"Of course I do, but the first time I felt the vibe it was in the motel room with Raskhan... I mean you. But I didn't know it was you."

"I know. Actually I counted on that."

Damn if that wasn't a confession of his deceiving her into believing he was his brother. And she wanted more of that!

"Why?"

"I needed you to believe I was Raskhan. That was the only way I could ensure your safety in both universes. Khord wanted your hide, and the council was about to send a tracking team. The last thing I wanted was for you to spend your life running away."

"I guess I am easy to fool, but how do you delude vampires? I mean Zontag told me your voice is unmistakably different from Raskhan's, and that's how they all tell you apart."

"True. Although nobody is aware that Raskhan and I mastered that difference by the time we were five years old. It started out as a game. You know, we were kids back then and excited to play pranks on Zontag. However, the ability to imitate each other's voice has proved extremely useful in the past few years. As it happens, we swap roles all the time."

"What for?"

Rogan ran both hands through his thick, dark hair. His gorgeous features showing the trust he placed in her, he resumed his explanation.

"The Overworld is a harsh place. Here in the palace you've seen the good side, but out there in the darkness it's a whole different story. Over the years, gangs of rogue vampires have formed. We've been able to stall them so far, but they're a constant threat to your world."

"In what way?"

"They refuse the Formula. Although it's nourishment enough for all of us, they want to feed on humans."

"Why?"

"The chase. The excitement. The kill."

Recalling the band of vampires who had sided with Khord, Liv shivered. She had seen the hungry look in their eyes, the hunter's stance about to kill a prey. With that in mind, she began to grasp Rogan's forbidding, domineering, and almighty attitude when he ruled. In such a dangerous universe, he had to show his authority at all times. He wasn't allowed to be king and lenient.

"I get that, but I'm sure Raskhan is a great king. Why does he have to rely on you to replace him?"

"Because we're half-human. Strictly speaking my brother is a minute older than me, but we've swapped places so many times that we're both kings of the Overworld. And we're also both deeply rooted to your world. As much as we belong here, we often need to cross over. It isn't a mere attraction, it's a part of our lives we need to fulfil."

"So when one of you is away, the other has to be king. Tell me something, does Zontag know?"

"No. We've never told anyone, it's the only way to avoid betrayal. Only you know our secret now."

When he said the words, a warm sensation quickened Liv's pulse. Although deceived like all the others, being trusted with their secret identities made her feel confident—and special in Rogan's eyes.

"When we first met, Khord called you a traitor to your race. I assume you wanted everyone to think that, but what's the point? I mean, why did you make all of them believe you hated your brother?"

"To ensure the king's sole authority. We were afraid someone might discover our secret so we came up with this idea. If we loathed each other, nobody would ever doubt Raskhan's identity and legitimacy. On the other hand, Rogan could come and go as he pleased without ever being questioned. Khord hated me on a personal level, and he was willing to use anything to declare me a traitor. Before he sided with rogues, I think he was the king's most faithful warrior. He never realised he fought with Raskhan a lot, convinced he was me."

As deeply as the monster vampire repulsed her, Liv wondered if killing him had been such a good move after all. Although thick-headed and vicious, Khord might still have had his uses.

"Did you want to kill him because he betrayed the king?"

Brow furrowed, Rogan shook his head. "I don't know why he went with rogues. We might have been able to get him back on our side, but he made the only mistake he shouldn't have."

"What's that?"

"He touched you."

A delicious heat spreading through her body, Liv stared at the intensity of the gaze stroking her face.

"Thank you for rescuing me. I've never been so afraid in my life."

"I know. I felt your fear. Just like when Khord tried to kill you in here, your fear guided me to you. And as I remember, you saved both me and my brother. We owe you our lives and our kingdom. By the way, nice trick you played on Khord and the other rogue."

Her grin matching his, Liv flapped her hand in a 'don't mention it' gesture. Yet Rogan was right, she had done an amazing thing there.

"Maybe it's my destiny. Maybe fate pushed you to me."

"I'm not sure. I've always thought we met by chance."

"When you smelt me in the store's parking lot?"

"Yes. Raskhan had gone on a trip to your world, but he should have been back home days earlier. I was getting worried, so I decided to pop over for a few hours and find him. Although I couldn't get out of taking Khord with me, I figured I'd find a way to give him the slip. I did for a while then he tracked me to the parking lot and, well, you know the rest. The thing is, I never imagined I would find you instead of my brother."

She had never imagined it either. For that matter, she had never envisioned meeting a vampire king and falling in love with him.

"Do you know how Raskhan got shot?"

"Earlier today, Raskhan went to your neighbourhood because he had picked up my scent. Figuring that I was still around, Khord and his trackers were also looking for me in the same area. He mistook my brother for me and shot him without warning. As he needed the council to witness a traitor's capture, and to prove his loyalty to the king, he had the body brought back here. After all, nobody could testify he had used a silver bullet. He was only doing his job."

Khord's 'job' had almost killed both brothers. A picture of the man she had then believed to be Rogan sprang to mind—face hollow, unconscious, and dying on a massage table.

"Why did you stop me when I tried to go heal your brother?"

"Because I needed you to do it. I figured you'd go anyway, but I knew you'd run to him if I forbade it. You're a stubborn little girl, Liv."

"Look, I understand your desperate need for secrecy, yet you could have confided in me. After our first night in the woods, you knew I'd never betray you. I'm sure you knew."

She wasn't making a wild guess. Rogan had endangered his safety and his secret for her. He was too responsible and powerful a king to risk an empire without good reason. Even back then he had known he could trust her, yet he had chosen to pretend to be Raskhan.

At this moment, Liv realised she had hit the mark when Rogan nodded. Taking his hands in hers, she looked at him straight in the eye, and spoke in her softest voice.

"Why didn't you tell me?"

In spite of her pleading gaze and tone, he still looked somewhat reluctant to give his reasons. Then he sighed, his mesmerising eyes seeming to caress her face.

"Because I wanted you to love me."

Chapter Thirty-Two

Startled, Liv blinked. Not a trace of deception or amusement in his eyes. Only truth and sincerity.

"I'm afraid I'm not following you there. When we parted at the warehouse, I was already in love with you."

"No, you weren't. You had a crush on the vampire who had saved your life, and that's not the same thing. I loved you."

"Hold on a second! Are you telling me what I was feeling?"

"As a matter of fact, I am."

Raising her eyebrows, Liv withdrew her hands. Although Rogan still knelt at her feet, she suddenly had the impression that he was towering over her — a mighty king ruling his house and his people. A dark vampire she had come to know as Raskhan.

"Well, you're wrong!"

"Are you sure about that? So far you had met Rogan, the interesting, thoughtful vampire who ignited your wildest fantasies. Don't get me wrong, I am that man. But I can also be sarcastic, scary, hurtful, violent, and cruel when I want to achieve something. And I am that man too."

"So?"

"So I wanted you to love me for who I really am, not to fulfil some exciting fantasy you had been dreaming of."

To her surprise, everything he was telling her rang true. He had figured her out way better than she had. Reflecting on their time together, Liv had to admit Rogan wasn't the man she had believed him to be before stepping into the Overworld.

As much as the realisation had cost her, she wouldn't lie to him. He had been playing a risky little game, but he had been right. As she opened her mouth to tell him, he raised a hand to silence her.

"Okay, let's pretend Rogan never existed. Can you honestly tell me you would have fallen in love with Raskhan? Have you already forgotten how I treated you as Raskhan? How I teased you, mocked you, threatened you, and played with your feelings? And how I get my kicks out of it?"

"Well, given time I might have…"

He ripped her robe apart. So quickly she didn't see him move, the robe was in tatters and dangerous shards glittered in his eyes.

"I don't have time for your fancies, little girl. Now, lie down!"

His abrupt harsh tone ignited in her a fit of rebellion. Just because he had gone out of his way to make her love him didn't mean she'd submit to his every mood. Stiffening her back, she defied him.

"The hell I will!"

A flicker of desire crossed his eyes as she resisted his will. Then he ripped off her underwear, grabbed her wrists, and held them behind her back with only one of his hands. As she gasped, her shock drew a sly grin on his face.

"Are you sure, kitten? I seem to recall you owe me some begging."

Flustered, she twisted her body. Not to get out of his firm grip on her, but to fight off the hot wave of desire setting her body alight. He had no right to treat her rough, yet she loved it.

"Let go of me."

"How about I do this instead?"

He stroked her thigh with his free hand—a slow, arousing caress from her knee right up to her bush. As she clamped her legs together he went for her sex, and pressed his stiff finger against her clitoris.

"Got you!"

His teasing grin unnerved her much less than the touch of his hand. Even without moving, his rogue attitude was turning her into a horny female. As if her body possessed a will of its own she felt hot and moist, she felt like his finger, drenched in her desire. He applied a slight pressure on her excited flesh, and she moaned.

"Oh, yes, kitten. You look so sexy when you moan for me."

Then he penetrated her with his whole finger, and of their own volition her legs came apart. As a man used to taking opportunities, he withdrew his digit to find her most sensitive spot. Tracing slow tight circles, he sent exciting flames leaping throughout her body. Unable to withstand the raw desire his finger fuelled, she let out a single sharp cry.

"What is it, little girl? Am I not pleasing you, or is it something else you want?"

When he rolled her nipple against the palm of his other hand, she realised he wasn't holding her wrists anymore, and probably hadn't been for a while. She couldn't have cared less as she had no intention of getting away from the torturing bliss of his finger. All she craved now was what he had promised she would some day beg for.

"Lick me."

His over-satisfied smile told her he had been thinking the same thing. Still, he didn't act on it but squinted as if something was missing.

"Come again? I'm not quite sure I heard begging."

"Because I won't beg."

Looking a little startled, he nevertheless kept on fondling her clit. Using her elbows to wrench herself away from him, she moved backwards to sit in the middle of the bed. Her eyes boring into his surprised gaze, she drew her knees up and spread her legs as far as she could. Her cunt wide open and glistening from desire, she commanded the king of the Overworld.

"I said suck me!"

Eyes widening, he put one of his hands on his crotch as if to relieve a painful tension. He didn't hesitate. The upper part of his body lying flat on the bed, he plunged his face between her thighs. His tongue grazed her so sensitive lips, and she clenched the sheet with both hands. Darting inside, his tongue flicked her clit a few times, and she sighed with contentment.

But when he kissed and licked her aroused flesh, she longed for more. She longed for him so violently she wondered if his touch would ever be too much. Bringing her hands to his head, she raised his beautiful face.

"Make love to me, Rogan. Suck me, fuck me, or do whatever you want with me. I love you."

As she spoke her true feelings, his eyes shone with passion and love. Using his vampire speed, it took him a literal second to discard his clothes and stand naked at the foot of the bed. Stretched towards her, his glorious erection seemed to plead for her wet sex. Then the king of the Overworld came to her on his knees.

Resting on her elbows, she watched him push his cock into her. Then she lay down to enclose his waist in the narrow ring of her legs. His rigid sex buried in her pussy, his sensual mouth right above her, he blew a lock of hair away from her eyes. His lips hovering over hers, his gaze glinted as he said something she hadn't expected to hear from him.

"Tell me you'll never leave me."

"I'll abandon you every time you tease me."

He grinned. Although he made no move, she could feel his sex throbbing in her cunt. He kissed her cheek before his lips slid down to her neck to lick the tiny scar, the soft spot where he had last bitten. The king's mark. Warm and firm, his mouth came up to her ear.

"But you'll come back?"

A little short of breath, enveloped in the luscious heat of his love, she tightened her leg grip.

"That depends on what my reward will be."

He arched his back to shove his dick deep into her. She shuddered, his sudden thrust grazing her clitoris and filling her to the brim. Letting out an excited sigh, she burrowed her nails in the muscles of his shoulders. Then he nibbled her earlobe with his teeth and whispered in her ear.

"A reward? Yes, I think we can reach an agreement. How about something like this, little girl?"

Straightening up to look at her, he began moving slowly inside her. As his stony dick sent relentless shots of pleasure throughout her body, his mouth came down on hers. All her senses sharpened by his hunger, his ravenous kiss blew her breath away. In and out, the regular beat of his cock drew her towards heavenly delights.

Born from the fire licking her loins, a long moan swelled within her throat only to be snapped up and swallowed by the brushing of his tongue. Her limbs trembled when he finally released her mouth. Her nails bit deeper into his shoulders as he slowed his rhythmic thrusts to look into her eyes.

"Is this what you had in mind?"

Lost in his gaze, she plastered her belly against his. His brief wince of pleasure had all her muscles twitching, and they both groaned while she slid her hands up to cup his face.

"Show me your fangs."

He did. His long white canines came down over his lower lip, and he loved her more profoundly than she'd have thought possible. And when his compulsion bested him he found that she had already bared the way to her neck.

Like the first time they had made love in the woods, he bent his face down. And, like the first time, his fangs drew blood from her throat as their cries reached their climax.

* * * *

Later that night, they talked about the Bringer of Death. Zontag's tests had proved Liv's blood was pure. In addition to the test results, her display of power over Khord and the rogue confirmed that she was the deadly threat of their legend. It didn't mean she would act accordingly.

She belonged to her sunny world, not to these barren, dark territories, and she had nothing to do here. If Rogan asked for her help she'd use her power to change rogue vampires into humans, but she had no desire to turn this world upside down. Thousands of years ago, it had been made this way for a reason. Who was she to decide a whole race had to be eradicated?

What weighed more on Liv's mind was the future of their relationship. Not easy to love a vampire king. But Rogan would cross over universes to be with her every time she wanted him, and sometimes she'd come to thoroughly enjoy his hot tub. Either here or in the world of the living they'd be together. Nothing else mattered.

Although pretty tired, Liv might have dwelt on it a little longer but he kissed her then and all rational thoughts disbanded. For the second time that night under Rogan's firm lips and probing tongue, she rediscovered the blazing sensations she had experienced when kissing him for the first time.

In the end, he had been right. Had he kissed her so brazenly when he was posing as Raskhan, she'd have recognised him in a heartbeat. But already her breasts were calling for his touch. Already her stomach was on fire and his erection seeking to enter her, to fill her with pure passion.

As Rogan deeply rooted himself inside her, Liv looked at his golden-freckled gaze. "Come on, my king, give me some more of your vampire love."

He shivered with desire. She closed her eyes.

About the Author

Chris Lange is a sensual romance author, and a dreamer. She daydreams, nightdreams, Mondaydreams, weekenddreams, springdreams, winterdreams. Then, she writes. Welcome to her fantasy world.

Chris Lange loves to hear from readers. You can find her contact information, website details and author profile page at http://www.total-e-bound.com.

Total-E-Bound Publishing

www.total-e-bound.com

Take a look at our exciting range of literagasmic™
erotic romance titles and discover pure quality
at Total-E-Bound.